TRADING VINCENT CROW

TRADING VINCENT CROW

D.C.J. WARDLE

Copyright © 2013 D.C.J. Wardle

The moral right of the author has been asserted.

Apart from any fair dealing for the purposes of research or private study, or criticism or review, as permitted under the Copyright, Designs and Patents Act 1988, this publication may only be reproduced, stored or transmitted, in any form or by any means, with the prior permission in writing of the publishers, or in the case of reprographic reproduction in accordance with the terms of licences issued by the Copyright Licensing Agency. Enquiries concerning reproduction outside those terms should be sent to the publishers.

Matador
9 Priory Business Park,
Wistow Road, Kibworth Beauchamp,
Leicestershire. LE8 0RX
Tel: (+44) 116 279 2299
Fax: (+44) 116 279 2277
Email: books@troubador.co.uk
Web: www.troubador.co.uk/matador

ISBN 978 1780883 267

British Library Cataloguing in Publication Data.
A catalogue record for this book is available from the British Library.

Typeset by Troubador Publishing Ltd, Leicester, UK

Matador is an imprint of Troubador Publishing Ltd

Printed and bound in the UK by TJ International, Padstow, Cornwall

For Jill

Chapter 1 – Washing up

New Year's Eve

Vince scraped the gunk from the bottom of the final saucepan with his water-wrinkled hand. He plunged it into the lukewarm, murky water of the sink and scrubbed half-heartedly at the bottom with a scourer. He was convinced that his boss wouldn't mistreat the pans, or use quite so many, if she was the poor bugger who had to wash them up afterwards. Natalie Sedgwick, who was both the cook of questionable bar-meals, and spouse of the pub's owner, was currently in the bar enjoying the New Year's Eve party. Vince imagined her, G&T in hand, flirting with the regulars. She would be laughing in an over-the-top way at their crude jokes whilst Dennis, her husband, polished glasses at the end of the bar, watching in silent annoyance and jealousy. She had about as much apathy towards Vince's desire for an easier run, as Vince had towards his current occupation. Delving into the depths of the industrial-sized sink, Vince located and removed the plug, watched the water slowly gurgle down, and then began to scrape more gunk and soggy bits of vegetable from around the plug hole. Natalie Sedgwick had a thing about her sink looking cleaner than the pots that were scrubbed in it.

Vince swept and mopped the floor of the kitchen. The muffled sounds of 70's Christmas classics accompanied the shouted conversations of people with better jobs than him, who didn't have to work on public holidays. Once he'd finished, he propped the broom up in the corner, he grabbed his coat and left via the back door which led into the car park. Having dumped the evening's black bag of soggy leftovers in the bins at the top of the car park, he began his walk home. Passing the front of the pub, he peered through the window at the drunken mob of revellers. He knew a lot of them. Through the frosted pane he could see Jenny Davis, a girl that he'd had a crush on throughout school. She was at the end of the bar getting-off with Dan Bridges, whom coincidentally he had also been at school with and despised with a passion. Jenny was now a receptionist at a car rental place. Dan worked on a till in a supermarket. Vince pondered at how amazingly pathetic a bunch of drunken people appear when you yourself are sober, and yet somewhere within him was a need to be as drunk and pathetic as them. After all, being wasted and getting off with Jenny Davis was the pinnacle of aspiration in small town life. It didn't get any better. The days in-between such fleeting moments of excitement were a monotonous drudgery, and it would never change. Jenny was not going to progress past receptionist. She neither had the drive, the skills or the opportunity. Indeed, her looks had probably helped her land the job and a younger, better looking girl would eventually come along and replace her. Meanwhile, Dan was always going to be a thug. He was a violent piece of work at school and was still a moron now. His strong jaw-line, rugged appearance and just enough money to buy attractive girls drinks would carry him along until he eventually got one of them pregnant and would have to get married. He'd then realise he actually had a naff job, a life which had acquired responsibilities, and then take out the frustrations of his wasted existence on his kids. Their offspring would in turn on go to become thugs and terrorise more sensitive kids at school. This was a circle of life that was rarely covered on in-depth documentaries.

As Vince crossed the road opposite the pub, he turned on hearing the front door of the pub swing open and two pissed-up, middle-aged women staggered out. The stagger was emphasised by their clothes that were a few sizes too small and rather impractical for the cold urban winter. Their make-up was applied liberally to evoke a message of availability. The first one immediately fell into a bush next to the porch. The second then screeched with laughter at an unnecessarily high volume. Having realised this noisy display had failed to attract any welcome attention from passing hunks, she knelt on the ground and began to throw-up loudly into a pot plant: damp soil and vomit no doubt making an unwelcome addition to the peroxide. Should these delightful ladies remember any of their display, a romanticised version of the incident would surely be their big story for many Friday nights to come. Vince looked through the open door at the groups of drunken party-goers. A week before he would have walked right in there and joined the crowd. He would have happily spent all the money he'd just earned whilst washing-up their dirty dishes trying to become part of the Jenny and Dan social group. He would eventually leave with less money and a similar social status to when he started, but the water-wrinkled hands from a night of washing up would remain.

Instead he walked straight past the pub and started down the road towards home with a wry grin spreading across his face. Vince Crow had been party to a revelation the day before, that was going to change his life forever. He was no longer one of the small town crowd that delighted in tales of vomiting into plant pots. Vince Crow was about to start living life differently.

The inspiration

Vince had been waiting at a bus-stop on the corner of the street. To pass the time he faced the only clean-ish bit of glass on the window of the closed shop behind the bus shelter. His simple aim was to see if he could thaw the frost in a variety of patterns with his warm breath. The rest of the glass window had clearly been the venue for a spitting contest that had provided entertainment for the preceding group of bus-waiters.

As the first signs of successful thawing began, two middle-aged women arrived to wait for the bus as well. They had seemingly reached a point in their life-journey where discretion and social embarrassment had been diminished, from years of yelling at small off-spring. A self-conscious approach to interaction in public places was no longer a valued attribute. For Vince, escape from their loud, bland conversation would be unachievable without abandoning the need to get the next bus.

The shared walk to the bus stop and the subsequent wait had eventually exhausted the ladies of all repetitive cooing over the pushchair-baby combination belonging to the first woman, and the evolving baby bump of the second – such was the infrequency of buses. In Vince's opinion, the chubby baby in the pushchair may well have been the inspiration, or even the winner, of the spitting contest that had preceded him at the window, judging by the gelatinous goo on its chin.

In the uncomfortable space that resulted from the first woman failing to loudly announce all that was passing through her mind, as nothing was passing, she moved on to the contents of a trashy magazine that was tucked into the back of the pushchair. Vince turned his attention to the back of the bus shelter, and started to peel at the corner of a poster of some bloke wearing a complicated-looking watch.

Having reviewed the gossip columns, and the blurred line between the reality and the TV lives of soap stars, the women moved on to an article about the internet. Despite neither having used a computer, they were intrigued that you could use it to swap or sell old stuff you didn't want and then order new stuff that you did. Old junk could be transformed into new money without having to leave your own home and place an ad in the classifieds. Vince had no interest in the internet, or the vocalisation of limited mental activity, which would be better if it remained unexpressed. It sounded a bit like the Saturday morning *Multi-coloured Swap-Shop* to him. From memory this was for kids that were allowed to use the phone, swapping their Scalextric for drum kits. At the time he had dismissed this gem of trading knowledge in favour of returning to the window and seeing if he had enough warm breath to un-freeze the word 'arse' on the glass before his bus arrived. The moment passed.

In contrast to verbally enthusiastic women at bus stops, Vince did have a job where he had far too much time to think about things, and these thoughts were destined to bounce around inside his head instead of being expressed to the world at large. After all, his main companion through his working existence was a Brillo Pad.

The memories of baby dribble and the internet conversation returned to him the next day, whilst scraping some black goo off the back of one of the pub's fridges with a dessert spoon. Trading up things of no value, and turning them into valuable assets was very much something for which he had the initial outlay required. The question was, what would he have to trade-up on the internet, and what did he expect to get back in return? Indeed, could he be bothered with the effort of following up on this at all? It seemed like you needed get very lucky, otherwise everyone would have already dropped their normal working lives in favour of this approach to financing their existence. Alternatively, you could spend a lot of time down at the post office wasting your four-pound-fifty an hour washing-up pittance on buying a lot of stamps, and swapping tat with other people who were also wasting stamps. This conundrum reminded him of the stories of gold rushes when the only people making money were the ones selling the shovels and sieves. In this modern day analogy, the answer was then to either open a post office, or start a stamp collection.

Then, just as Vince decided that the dessert spoon was bending out of shape too much to be able to bend it back again, and that he'd be better off with a bread knife, he had a moment of lateral thinking that was about to re-shape his life. Why trade-up 'stuff' to get more and better stuff. It was still just going to be stuff, but more of it. Despite having slightly more stuff, he was still going to be stuck in the same dead-end job. An occupation which seemed to revolve around removing material that may have once been edible, but had since decomposed into something slightly alien, and had cemented itself to various inaccessible parts of a kitchen. With sufficient devotion to the internet and the postal service, his room in the house where he lived with his nan could eventually contain a big-size TV, or similar. However, he would still be basically the same person, with the same mediocre looks and personality. He would still be a person who would continue to go to the same bars each week with not much money, and fail to attract the likes of Jenny Davis. No, trading stuff was not the answer. And then it struck him. What he was going to have to do, was trade himself.

Right now Vince was a washer-upper in a slightly run-down kitchen, in a slightly run-down suburban pub. This washer-upper had to be traded up for something better, and that something better would then be traded upwards again and again until he was the man he needed to be. The more Vince thought about it, the more it made sense. It wasn't going to be just about trading jobs. Plenty of people did that. It was called 'a career', and not something that happened to college drop-outs who washed-up in knackered pub kitchens. No, this was a lifestyle thing. At each stage he would have to trade-up the lot. The job, the girl, the wheels, the pad, the threads – everything.

With every step upwards the whole of his life had to change upwards, and for the better. Fortunately, at least in terms of this ambitious process, he currently had no wheels, no girlfriend, and his clothes were old and hole-ridden. In fact he barely had what he considered to be 'a job'. This meant that getting to the next step would be fairly straight forward. After all, what he did have was a plan, and that was something Danny Bridges was never going to have.

The threads

New Year's Day arrived, and so had 'day one' of the first trade-up. Having thought about it thoroughly over several days, Vince had decided that trade-up number one would mean becoming a barman. He had current experience in the catering trade – and by extension the hospitality business. He also had a lot of knowledge about drinking, being an enthusiast himself to some degree, and he had an A-level in Physics which could look impressive on a CV so long as he didn't mention the grade. Now all he needed was the image. He was currently a washer-upper and, consequently, he looked like one. He turned up to work each lunchtime and evening in some grubby jeans and an old T-shirt. These were clothes that wouldn't matter when he returned home, stinking of chip fat and stained with anything that had spilled, dripped, splashed or attached irreversibly to him as he was cleaning out the inside of the bins. However, there was a barman job going at The Carrot and Jam Kettle where he was currently a reliable employee, and today he would need to convince the owners that he was the man for the job.

It was with more clarity than he had exuded for several years that Vince rose at an early hour with a spring in his step, and a hangover that was completely absent. It was time to head to the new-year sales. A fresh set of clothes was going to be his opening gambit with which he would trade into the barman business. He would then give himself three months to use this new rung on the ladder of power to trade-up for a lifestyle that was even better.

He had never been to the January sales before and was amazed at the intensity of the shoppers and the single-mindedness of them to achieve a bargain. Uninhibited bus-stop women paled in comparison to the enthusiastic crowd that were ready to draw blood if they failed to save a couple of quid on something they didn't really need. They hung around the locked doors of unopened stores, their breath hitting the cold air and forming a mist. Dragon-like qualities were stirring in the tension and anticipation as the scent of battle filled their runny and snivelling nostrils. The fact that the items in the sales were a bargain seemed to take precedence over whether they were actually any good or even wanted. Vince felt smug in the knowledge that his bargains were not only wanted, but were in fact essential to a higher goal. This raised his confidence, and he started to feel a bit superior to the simpletons that were jostling for position and waiting for the high street shops to open their doors.

That afternoon, Vince returned up the hill towards his nan's house with carrier bags of carefully selected shirts and trousers, and a pair of leather shoes. These were multi-purpose garments. Firstly, they would achieve their primary aim, and impress as a barman uniform. Also they would impress customers at the bar who could be the key businessmen, and the sources of opportunities for future trade-ups. He would get access to new and better things as he networked. Fumbling in his pocket he found the key to the front door of the run-down terrace house. The sticky lock required a few attempts, as usual, until eventually it gave up the fight and performed the task it was designed for. Vince pushed open the stubborn door against the weight of fliers and free papers that were accumulating behind it.

Before heading up the stairs to his room, Vince peered in the direction of the grubby kitchen where his grandmother was sitting in front of an electric fire and nursing a mug of what was probably stewed tea.

"Yaw alright Nan?" he called.

"The second bar's on the pissin' blink again."

The reply from the disgruntled woman was then followed by her kicking the side of the small electric heater with her slipper-clad foot. Whether this was to help Vince with some enlightment of what she was referring to, an attempt to correct the fire's current level of utility, or as a general expression of frustration and contempt for the item, Vince wasn't sure. He chose to respond with a non-sequitur himself to avoid being drawn into the heater discussion any further.

"Back from the shops, Nan. I'll be upstairs."

The statement seemed to achieve its aim and he headed towards his room before any new discussion about either the heating arrangements or his purchases could kick in.

Vince was so inspired by the fact that he had started his trading plan that he changed immediately into one of his new outfits. The black trousers teamed with a white shirt. The subtle blue stripes were classy but not over the top, business-like, and said that he was a man with confidence. He decided he would wear it to work so that he could pitch himself to Dennis and Natalie Sedgwick as their new barman. There was no time like the present. After all, he had to become a barman, succeed at it, and then trade-up to something else in three months or less.

A bit more deodorant, some hair gel to semi-tame his curly black locks, and Vince headed back down the creaky stairs. He took his coat from the end of the banister, and decided to share some kind words with his gran before heading out in to the cold wastelands.

"Off to work now, Nan," he volunteered as a parting gesture, should she need to be keeping a running total of the occupancy of the house.

"That Mrs Garret has taken her pissin' net curtains down, and you can see right inside her front room. It's all green and posh lamps and that. Just rubbin' in how much pissin' money they've got."

Vince was used to his nan's conversation simply being the out-loud version of her disjointed train of thoughts, and didn't feel the need to reply. If the Mrs Garret brought to his attention in this outburst was located in the same shabby street as them, then the wealth issue was all somewhat relative, regardless of what sort of lamps you had in your green living room. He pulled the door hard behind him so that it would stay closed, whilst carefully holding only the handle so that the pealing blue paint wouldn't come off on his new threads. He then headed up the street toward his new and improved destiny. The spring in his step was slightly curtailed by the first wearing of his new shoes, and quickly took the form of a cautious shuffle. Having worn trainers for years he'd forgotten how slippy a cheap pair of shoes could be, especially on an icy path. He was also quickly reminded how new shoes rubbed blisters into your heels as well. It was like being back in school.

The interview

Vince pushed open the front door of The Carrot and Jam Kettle with as much confidence as he could muster. He strode towards the bar where Natalie lounged, like a lizard that had applied foundation but with only a 30-watt bulb to support the process. Both she and her cleavage seemed to be sharing a similar degree of interest in a glossy magazine as they both peered down at it with great intensity.

"Yaw alright there Nat?"

It was a reasonable opening gambit considering the unremarkable nature of the circumstances. Natalie looked up from her magazine, and smirked at the all new Vince that stood before her.

"A bit tired after all the partying last night. What's with the new get-up?"

"I wanted to apply for the barman job – I saw the ad in the front window. Is Dennis about?"

"Dennis is down at his mother's place. The old witch! Why he needs to be rushing down there at the beck and call of that old hag I'll never know. D'yaw know last time I was there she looked me up and down and actually raised her eyebrows at me before I'd even made it through the front door. I said to Dennis, I said, if your mother is going to take that kind of attitude you can bloomin' well go there on your own next time. And the cakes she makes. They're like bloomin' rocks. You need a dental appointment after a cup of tea round there."

"Right... So, what d'you think then?"

"About what?"

"The barman job?"

"Well we are a bit short-staffed tonight. In fact, I'm expecting a quiet one so I thought I'd do the bar myself tonight like, and not bother to do meals. D'yaw know anything about being a bartender, Vince? How to pull pints, work the till, mix drinks and that?"

"I know how to do all the different drinks. Besides, when you send me into the bar for fetching a drink to the kitchen for you, Dennis usually tells me to sort it out by me-self like. He usually gets me to change the barrels over as well. The till should be okay. I'm not thick y'know. Got an A-level, so I can do the maths in me head if I had to."

"Let's give you a try out then. You can't be any worse than the last girl we had in here. All boobs and no brains. Bloomin' hopeless tart."

Vince concentrated hard at controlling the muscles in his head so that his eyebrows didn't automatically rise up like those of Natalie's mother-in-law. The reason for Kassie's early dismissal from The Carrot and Jam Kettle was not so much due to the lack of brains but more due to the former attribute mentioned. They had clearly been influential in Dennis's recruitment decision-making process regarding the girl, and Natalie was clearly unable to tolerate the competition. When Dennis, or any other lonely punters, glanced up and caught sight of a slightly tarty woman behind the bar with an excessive cleavage, it was either going to be Natalie that made them drool, or no-one.

"Let's show you the ropes then."

Natalie manoeuvred herself from the bar-stool where she perched, with the air of someone trying to be delicate, and led Vince behind the bar. After a ten minute explanation of the system, where the drinks were, what they cost, which optics and which glasses to use, a further five minute explanation of the till meant that Vince's training was complete.

Natalie returned to her stool, taking with her the example gin and tonic from the training, along with the example Campari and soda and the example rum and Coke. Those whom it affected returned to the glossy magazine, and Vince started to clean the glasses. This was already a rung up the ladder for Vince. The glasses had their own very clean dish-washer which required loading up, pressing a button and waiting for clean glasses to return. No scrubbing or gunk, or plungers required. The pay would probably be better too, though he'd not thought to negotiate it. At the time of his appointment to bartender, his sharp analytical mind had decided that he'd achieve the position based on the apathy from Natalie toward working herself that evening. Normally she was in her element when flirting with the punters and screeching in an annoying way at weak and inappropriate jokes about sex. These were invariably told by middle-aged married men, who couldn't see the irony that they were sat in a group of men, filling in the time before returning to a stale marriage where exciting sexual capers were far from being on the menu.

At 7.00pm a couple of old guys came in for their usual Sunday evening drink that had now become a Tuesday evening drink on account of the New Year holidays. Vince successfully provided each of them with a pint of Best, and used the till correctly when he charged them for it. They took up their normal position at a corner table, where they stared at the beer hoping it would magically start a conversation, as they hadn't brought one of their own.

Natalie had been right. It was a quiet evening, after all it was a Tuesday, the average pub-goer would be recovering from partying to early hours the day before, and most people had to return to work the next day. It was the perfect opportunity for Vince to quietly learn the ropes. Natalie remained at her barstool whilst Vince continued to serve some high-ball drinks to a couple and some more pints to the locals, who had made it in on principle. By 10.00pm the bar was empty except for Natalie and Vince. Vince had collected up the last of the glasses from the tables and was doing a final batch in the dishwasher. Natalie was downing her fourth martini.

"His mother's never liked me, y'know!"

Vince looked up at Natalie from across the bar. This sudden out-burst from nowhere was a bit like having a conversation with his nan.

"She's a meddling old cow! Pour me a double vodka would you Vincent. Have one yourself an' all!"

Vince obeyed and took the drinks over to where Natalie was resident at the end of the bar. He'd seen in movies that bartenders are also supposed to take on a psychologist role, listening and apparently caring about all the sad drunks and their irrelevant problems. Clichés like 'a penny for your thoughts' were supposed to spring forth from his lips as a natural part of his being.

"Everything alright with yaw Nat? You seem a bit upset, like."

"No, everything isn't all right, Vince."

Natalie's hissed reply contained the poisonous vapour of several martinis, gin, rum and vodka, which hit Vince as hard as the shock of the reply itself.

"He walked out didn't he. He'd gone this morning without so much as a 'good bye and sorry I was such an arsehole last night' !"

Natalie paused, to enable Vince the opportunity to enquire further. Vince really wasn't sure he wanted to enquire further. It struck him that his new career may be based on the recruitment by a drunk middle-aged woman, who had been abandoned within the last twenty-four hours by the man who had the real clout in terms of hiring and firing bartenders at The Carrot and Jam Kettle.

"Last night he accused me. Accused *me* mind you, of flirting with Nigel Salmon from the dentists. Can yaw believe it? I told him he was a right one to talk considering he couldn't get his eyes of Kassie James for more than thirty seconds. He only bloomin' stormed off. I thought he was just having one of his sulks. This morning he was gone. Off crying to mummy if you ask me."

Vince nodded sympathetically as he watched Natalie scull the remains of her double vodka. This was not how he had hoped his first day of the new career would be going.

"Right Vincey. I plan to drink my way across the optics – and I'm not doing it alone. We'll start on the left with the Cinzano and work across to the Jack Daniels on the right. Well then, don't just stand there. Get a wriggle on. Go and get a couple of fresh glasses."

Vince obeyed. *Do what your boss asks and you can't go wrong,* he thought to himself, as he downed his Cinzano and ventured back to the optics for the next vermouth on the list. He'd never really been one for the more cocktail type of shots and felt it was a shame that they'd not started in the scotch section while he was still sober enough to appreciate them. Starting at the martini end it was unlikely they'd get as far as the single malts looking at the state that Natalie was in. However, she was known as a bit of a drinker so she shouldn't be underestimated.

Dennis Sedgwick

Dennis: proprietor, founder and licensee of The Carrot and Jam Kettle, sat in a comfortable chair at his mum's house, drinking his favourite scotch. He was enjoying the relative calm that correlated exponentially with increased physical distance from his wife. Jealousy was just one of the cruel mistresses that he endured. The others included his wife and his mother. He had been contemplating the events of the previous evening for some time, and was gradually forming a theory about the boundaries that his so-called wife was allowed to cross. Some handsome young tearaway making eyes at his wife was actually okay with him, as long as it didn't go further. His ego was boosted by the fact that at the end of the night the good-looking wannabe would leave on his own, and he would eventually go upstairs with Natalie feeling smug. However, Natalie's flirtations with Nigel Salmon were beyond comprehension. Nigel was older, pudgier, more bristly, more bald-spotty, and had at least one more chin than Dennis. Therefore, following the logic that a better man failing to snatch away his woman was an ego boost, Nigel Salmon making any kind of progress towards his incumbent was quite the opposite. That miserable sod was going to regret flirting with his wife, and his Natalie was going to learn her place.

Sipping his scotch and staring at some game show on the TV without taking in a word of it, Dennis's thoughts drifted to Natalie. She and the pub, and therefore his life, were basically inseparable. Dennis was essentially a beer-drinking armchair football pundit, as well a terrible gossip. It was therefore by no means an accident that he had become a barman. His sports trivia knowledge knew no bounds, and he mainly failed his A-levels because the academic school year and the football season had greatly overlapped. However, he would never have got into the trade if it had not been for Natalie's influence. They first met at a house party somewhere near the Student Union at Luton Polytechnic, as it was then known. To Dennis's half-cut mind when he first spied Natalie across the densely smoky room, he saw a young woman with a full-ish figure, but not fat, an attractive face and yet not stunning, and someone who was both absolutely rat-arsed and unspoken for. The last two facts were the deal-clincher that ensured he was luckier than the people that owned the coats that had been piled on the bed. Dennis was working evenings in a bar around the corner from where Natalie had a room in a student flat. The next night she sat at the bar, Dennis furnished her with cheap drinks all evening and then they returned to her place. This was particularly convenient for Dennis as it took two buses or a £6.00 taxi ride to get to his flat. This alone, in the absence of Natalie, made the job slightly unsustainable. For the first four months of their courtship, Dennis had never had a sober conversation with Natalie.

Dennis smiled at the memory and poured himself another scotch. Maybe he had over-reacted. Natalie was a flirt, but that helped pull in a few punters – there was no harm in it. No, deep down Natalie was loyal and devoted. About a year ago they'd vaguely talked about having a baby. At least Natalie had. He'd managed to wriggle out of the conversation on the basis that he got tickets to see Wolverhampton play West Brom at home. Of course Natalie's maternal needs had never come to anything. They both worked unsociable hours running the pub and there was no time for that sort of thing. Now he thought about it, maybe their relationship did need a bit more to it. Some children perhaps, to make their bond stronger? Was now the time? Yep, maybe it was. He'd go back in the morning, flowers in hand, apologise unreservedly and they'd start making the babies that Natalie presumably craved.

The slight misdemeanour

Vince gradually became aware of his own consciousness. He started off by being aware that he was no longer asleep, which is not necessarily the same thing as being awake. He then gradually eased his way down that long bleak journey of becoming aware that a decision's been made to dig up the high street using a pneumatic drill, but for some reason it's happening inside your head. A feeling of sickness was building up as well. Past experience told Vince that standing up in order to get to a bathroom (which may or may not be nearby) would almost guarantee that he would be sick. Meanwhile, simply lying still for several hours could sometimes remove the problem altogether. He chose to remain horizontal and hide from the morning light from behind closed eyes. In his state of half-consciousness he gave a gentle caress to Natalie's soft wavy hair, as her head lay on his bare chest, gently breathing in easy slumber.

Vince immediately had one of those moments, for which there should be a scientific term, when a large number of thoughts rush through your mind all at once resulting in immense panic combined with an uncontrollable level of physical energy. The thoughts, in no particular order, included: *What? Who? Where am I? and Oh My God, Natalie! Dennis! What have I done!?* The physical energy dissipated itself via an incomprehensible yell that sounded a bit like the incantations of a startled wildebeest and Vince leaping vertically upward from Dennis and Natalie's purple sofa. He then rushed over to the window, opened it, stuck his head out of it, and hurled straight onto the beer barrels below.

Natalie had been sleeping peacefully. She suddenly woke to find that she was mid-journey in a violent sideways, catapulting manoeuvre between her sofa and the coffee table. Almost immediately the journey was over. The chain of events meant that the coffee table took up the relay's baton and careered into the MFI self-assembly bookcase. Natalie opened her eyes just in time to watch a precariously placed vase of flowers totter and then crash onto the television set. The overloaded extension lead to the side of the TV, which was less than impressed with the water from the exploding vase, gave a quick sizzle to vent its opinion. All that was attached to it, including the standard lamp, DVD player and stereo, then ceased to contribute actively to the functioning of the room. Through the blurred vision of the morning after, Natalie managed to raise her head to assess the bottom half of a hazy figure, leaning out of her lounge window and vomiting musically onto a selection of empty beer barrels below.

First encounters

Natalie's first encounter with Dennis Sedgwick was in the late summer of 1975, at the Henry Trowbridge Veterinary Clinic. Natalie, aged eight, was the proud owner of Henrietta, a small tortoise who for the previous three weeks had been looking increasingly depressed. Henrietta had been decidedly off her lettuce leaves – even the iceberg lettuce which had been bought at the weekend as a special treat to cheer her up. Natalie had tirelessly followed the advice provided by her *Blue Peter* annual in the care of household tortoises. It was too early for Henrietta to be considering hibernation, and so this could not be the explanation for the tortoise's total air of apathy to both Natalie and life in general. After vast amounts of pestering from Natalie, her mother had finally agreed to take Henrietta to see the vet.

Dennis, aged eleven, was also at the Henry Trowbridge Veterinary Clinic with his mother. They were accompanied by their over-active Yorkshire Terrier called Ruffles. Ruffles was being taken on a much needed de-worming mission. Over the previous two days he had caused various degrees of hilarity and despair, due to sitting on the new lounge carpet and dragging himself along with his front paws, whilst in a sitting position, to ease the itchiness of his worm-ridden hind-quarters. Having tried this technique on the tiled floor of the vet's waiting room, and finding it both difficult and unrewarding, Ruffles turned his attention to the small cage dangling precariously on the knees of the girl who was sitting next to him. Specifically the odour of the green rock on the other side of the bars was of particular interest. Unaware of Ruffles' presence, this was the moment that Henrietta decided that she would peer out of her shell for the first time that day to inspect her current environment. Ruffles spotted a head appearing from inside the rock and with the well-honed instinct of all good terriers, his reaction was to snap frantically at Henrietta. As a result, Ruffles snagged one of his teeth on the cage as he simultaneously got whacked over the head with a much loved, and potentially lethal, Sindy doll wielded by Natalie. Henrietta, who in the absence of any feet outside of her shell, had slid to the back of the cage and was thoroughly distressed by the entire event. Subsequently she refused to make any further attempt at an appearance for five full days. This made the vet's job slightly more difficult, and necessitated a return visit for Natalie and the tortoise later the following week. Ruffles was not only de-wormed but accumulated additional expense for the dental surgery that was now necessary.

The paths of Dennis and Natalie did not cross again for twelve years, and to this day they remain haplessly unaware of their original auspicious meeting.

The discussion

"To be perfectly honest Nat, I can't remember anything from last night past the double-shot of Malibu."

Fortunately, Vince's Midlands-borne voice had a naturally apologetic tone to it, which served him well in situations where things were not going as they should. He sipped guiltily at his mug of tea which was still far too hot to drink properly. Normally a glass of Coke was his first port-of-call in a hangover situation. However, making tea was the standard national response in the event of an emergency so he had little choice but to join Natalie in a brew.

Vince had managed to retain the basic facts of recent events, but there were a lot of gaps. He had woken up in nothing but his underwear, sharing a sofa with an equally under-dressed woman asleep on top of him. This was a woman who was his boss, and had recently promoted him. She was married to a man who was also his boss, although that boss didn't know he was his barman. Vince also had a big enough headache to bring back memories of getting paralytic the night before. However, the period of time between downing the Malibu last night and the morning event of pebble-dashing the car park was a complete mystery. At best, they'd got drunk, she'd told him he could take the spare-room but they'd innocently collapsed on the sofa before reaching their separate destinations. In this scenario, both would have been undressing on the way to their separate rooms; presumably to save time, but both somehow lost consciousness around the area of the sofa. At worst he'd made mad passionate love with Dennis's wife on his new purple sofa which had been recently bought with interest-free credit from DFS. This was a boss who was yet to learn that Vince was his new barman. Dennis's discovery of either version of events wasn't going to add to his enjoyment of Saturday afternoon footie, for which the lounge suite had primarily been acquired. Vince decided that neither scenario was an ideal position to find himself in on day two on the trade-up plan. Scenario number two however, on the face of it, did seem considerably worse.

Natalie's first experience of the morning had been the sight of Vince's Y-front clad rear-end, whilst the majority of him was dangling out of view, beyond where the hanging baskets went in the summer. Natalie's subsequent revelations, of which there were several, included acknowledgement that she too was dressed in only her underwear.

"Well, I can't even remember the bloomin' Malibu!"

Natalie's reply came after a considerably long silence. It wasn't one of those 'comfortable' silences that the heroes of tacky romantic comedy films delight in, having finally bonded for eternity with someone who was thought to be out of their league. No, this was an awkward silence of the type that has skin crawling for days after, at the merest recollection. It was true that there was always a negative correlation between Natalie's rate of alcohol consumption and her short-term memory. Her ability to recall what she had said or done diminishing with the number of vodkas taken, was a well-established mathematical phenomenon at The Carrot and Jam Kettle. However, the certainty of this outcome in this particular case wasn't to the benefit of the situation.

Natalie and Vince sat at opposite ends of the breakfast table. A distressed bunch of vase-less chrysanthemums lay scattered between them. Neither party was prepared to ask the question that hung between them like a sword of Damocles. A sword that couldn't make up its mind which of the two Damocles to dangle over first, and so had aimed for the chrysanthemums instead. Both of them were considering the consequences of the possible answer and neither were wanting to hear it. The bottom line was that neither Vince nor Natalie had a clue what had happened the night before. Indeed, there were only two possible courses of action to take and Vince decided it was time to take control.

"I reckon if you tidy up the vase, Nat, I'll get the hose out and wash down the vomit off them barrels."

Plan into action

By lunchtime the barrels had been cleaned, the living room in the flat above the pub had been re-aligned, and various electrical fuses had been replaced. The chrysanthemums were restored to their original position but in a different vase. Natalie was confident that Dennis wouldn't notice the difference, because he was a man. Should his DVD about Wolverhampton Wanderers look like it had been moved to a less prominent place on the DVD shelf, then this of course would be quite a different matter.

Vince was quietly skulking behind the bar, cleaning a large number of shot glasses. His audience of one was an aging local called Trevor, who seemed to be using his half-empty pint of beer as a magnifying glass to read the paper behind it. Natalie was apparently trying to keep a low profile in the kitchen, despite an obvious lack of food orders. However, it was just as Natalie emerged into the bar area with a bowl of chips to help Trevor process his second pint of mild, that Dennis burst enthusiastically through the main doors.

'Burst' was the word all right. Dennis was not a thin man due to years of having a quick pint with many a customer, and a diet featuring a high percentage of pork scratchings. His exercise routine extended to changing over the barrels and then returning up the stairs from the cellar out of breath. However, his usual challenge of navigating his frame through the pub doors was made all the more cumbersome by an enormous white fluffy rabbit, struggling to remain tucked under his arm. The hand of his other arm held a large blue plastic bag, making the operation of a door handle all the more tricky. For some reason the big grin on Dennis's face seemed to make him look slightly wider as well.

"Natalie!"

Fortunately Natalie looked up, shortly after depositing the basket of chips in front of Trevor. A moment earlier and they could have been in his lap. Dennis abandoned Flopsy, and in a rare moment of spontaneity rushed over to embrace the wife that he had recently abandoned.

"Oh Nat, I'm soo sorry!"

From the other side of the hug, Natalie looked with concern towards Vince who was trying to keep a low profile over by the glass washer. They still hadn't confronted the previous night's events with any kind of sensible conversation. And now this.

Dennis released Natalie from the bear-hug and stared deep into her eyes with his own blood-shot gaze, before dropping the bomb-shell.

"You an' me, Nat. We'm gonna have a baby!"

Natalie's expression of vague shock, combined with remnants of hang-over, changed immediately to one of complete shock. However, before she could react verbally to the announcement, Dennis held up his blue plastic bag triumphantly, and produced an article from within it.

"Look Nat, I've bought socks!"

Dennis was no fool. He'd sat through enough rubbish on the TV to know that the best way to finalise the deal on whether or not to have a baby is to show a woman a very, very small sock. Preferably the garment should have the image of something cute on the side, but this was not essential. His tiny socks had baby rabbits, to match Flopsy the rabbit who was now draped on a small round table near the bar with its left ear in an ash-tray. It turned out that Dennis was a master at psychological reinforcement. Natalie immediately went all gooey.

"Arr Dennis! I carn' believe it!"

Trevor started clapping, and Dennis gave the flushed and emotional Natalie a kiss before retrieving his giant rabbit and leading his gooey wife and their gooey plush rabbit upstairs. Vince returned from the shadows. Dennis, in his enthusiasm, had clearly failed to spot that Vince was now the new bar-tender at The Carrot and Jam Kettle. All things considered, there was actually no great hurry to let him know.

"What about that then! I should think this calls for a celebration!"

Trevor had returned to the bar, and confidently presented his empty pint glass, containing half a soggy chip in the bottom. He clearly assumed that a free drink on the house was at least implied in Dennis's shock announcement, if not actually communicated directly. Vince refilled Trevor's glass with a beer and didn't bother to charge him. In the absence of a financial demand from Vince, Trevor decided not to complain that the chip was still in there and was disintegrating to form a layer of mush near the top. The mind and concentration of Vince was on much bigger things than Trevor's daily quest to get free beer, that was also free from the results of the deep-fat fryer. The horror of what had just played out before him was just beginning to sink in.

The girl

Much to her surprise, Jenny Davis had not spent the start of the New Year having regrettable and drunken sex with Danny Bridges. This had been very much her misguided intention when she left The Carrot and Jam Kettle sometime after midnight. She and Dan had abandoned the pub as the New Year's Eve celebrations were deteriorating to less than successful demonstrations of 'Agadoo'. However, Dan had insisted that they stop off on their way back to her place, and look in on another party that a mate of his from work was throwing.

The party was okay. Jenny had mingled. Due to her good looks she was never in a position where she found herself embarrassingly on her own, which is a major social disaster at such events for those it affects. After realising that Dan had been gone far too long in his quest for the bathroom, she eventually abandoned the rather dull conversation she'd been stuck in at the bottom of the stairs with a guy called Mick who fitted kitchens, and went to look for him. She soon discovered that Dan had indeed made it to the bathroom successfully, but was actually still in there having sex in the empty bath-tub with Alison Bishop. She delivered a number of expletives to the bath-tub occupants and went home on her own, never to finalise her education from Mick on the best way to disguise a water heater behind Formica panelling.

Jenny Davis had been a typical girl at high school who was comfortable with her place in the 'attractive' set. This meant that she would only be friends with equally attractive girls, and they would then only go out with boys that were either good at football or rugby and whose parents were going to buy them a respectable looking car when they passed their test. The ultimate status symbol was to get a boyfriend who fitted these criteria but was in the year above. When time permitted from the busy schedule of these pursuits, Jenny and her attractive friends had the civil obligation to look down in a condescending manner at the rest of the kids who were either rubbish at sport, battling against a daily onslaught of acne, or just socially inept. Jenny was very much a success in this regard and had excelled at all of her socially-charged, high-school goals.

Having achieved two very poor A-levels, she then interviewed for receptionist at Gary's Car Rentals. Her timing couldn't have been better. Gary had been concerned for a while that Judith, his receptionist, was getting a little bit old. Her skin was aging prematurely due to her smoking and going on sunbathing holidays, from which she returned bright orange. This was not going to be a pull factor for clients looking to hire the top-range cars, however much lipstick she applied. Besides which, she had become rather too comfortable in her job, and no longer made any effort to flirt with Gary to help to confirm to his ego that he was still the most good-looking man on the small industrial estate.

At the interview, Jenny had responded to Gary's enthusiastic greetings with a flirtatious smile. She had fluttered her eye-lids after all of his poorly structured questions, giggled at his jokes, and had worn a short skirt. Judith's days were, alas, numbered. As time went on, unlike Judith, Jenny had at least had the sense to continue to remember why she had been hired. After all, it was not based on her grade D in A-level Art. Subsequently she had remained at Gary's Car rentals for nearly three years without Gary getting the itch to replace her.

Jenny had spent the majority of New Year's Day moping around in her PJs, when she arrived at something of a revelation of her own. Why was she worrying about being abandoned by Dan Bridges? A man, if you could call him that, who had abandoned her on the stairs to be lectured by a drunken kitchen-fitter about sprung cabinet hinges, so that he could shag Alison Bishop in a lime-green bath-tub. Surely Jenny deserved much better. It was time to find a good man and settle down. Her days of one-nighters with handsome guys, who discarded her when they were bored with her giggling, were over. Maybe she should look for someone whose plain looks and lack of athletic prowess meant that she wouldn't normally give them a second thought. She had reached that time in her life where she would look outside of her league of 'prettiness' for someone who was reliable and had a steady job to pay the rent. Someone who could support her and the mortgage for a detached house on the new estate so she didn't have to live with her mother.

Self-confidence

Jenny Davis was sitting at the end of the bar. She was looking pretty, but not too tarty. More notably she was sitting on her own, and Vince had just served her with a Malibu and Coke. This had been quite a physical under-taking in itself. Regardless of the challenge of serving someone he had fancied to the point of obsession whilst at high school, the smell of the Malibu had suddenly become completely repugnant to him. The mere sight of the bottle gave him convulsions. He suspected that he knew why this was the case, and decided that he was learning a lot about psychology at this brief period in his life. It was the first time that he and Jenny had spoken since high school. In fact, he wasn't entirely sure they had really ever spoken in high school, which may now be very much to his advantage. He did remember her laughing at him in unison with her similarly attractive blonde friends about his school trousers being too short. He was going to have to use that as the most recent point of contact in the absence of a more pleasant memory.

Meanwhile, returning to the present day, Jenny had just been very polite to him, and asked him how he was, as if they were old friends. Vince was rather taken back by this as he was anticipating a taunt about his new clothes or his job or something. In fact, Vince could swear she was flirting with him, and as a result he was very suspicious indeed. After all, at school Jenny might well have had her attractive-looking girly agenda. However, it should not be over-looked that all of those who were either rubbish at sport, battling against a daily onslaught of acne, or just socially inept, were very much aware of the agenda. None of the victims were ever as impressed as those dishing it out believed they should be.

The bar was returning to its usual level of custom. Despite this, Dennis and Natalie hadn't been down to the bar all evening. There was evidence that Dennis had decided to start on his project right away. Vince had heard the faint squeaking of bed-springs as he had passed the bottom of the stairs on the way to fetch a fresh box of cheese and onion crisps from the pantry.

Vince had put a notice on the bar saying that there were no meals tonight, and Trevor, who was still present, had made sure that all of the locals understood why.

There were about twenty to thirty customers in the pub and Vince felt he was doing well to manage things. It turned out he was pretty good as a bartender and regretted that he hadn't gone for the career move sooner. Maybe it was this new sense of self-confidence that was also having the inexplicable effect on Jenny Davis. During his delivery of the second Malibu and Coke, she had asked him about his job, what his hours were, and how much he was on. This was classic small talk as far as Vince was concerned, from the perspective of a man whose experience of small talk was relatively small. Vince didn't know how much he was on as he'd yet to be paid, so gave a figure that was double the washing-up rate. She'd looked impressed and had then offered to buy him a drink. He'd gone for a Coke on the pretext that he shouldn't be taking alcohol at work. Of course that was nonsense when you looked to Dennis Sedgwick as a role model for bartendering. However, Vince's head was still a bit muggy from the night before. Also, the smell of Malibu was becoming a serious deterrent against ever drinking again.

The bar had quietened a bit and Vince actually found himself in conversation with Jenny. This was indeed a triumphant moment of the first trade-up. Washing-up-Vince would never have been so courageous. They had been talking about a new movie and Jenny had suggested that she and Vince should go see it the next night. Vince had agreed. He didn't know if he was supposed to be working at the bar the next night. However, Dennis still didn't know that Vince was working behind the bar at all, so on that logic he was unlikely to be missed. Trade-up number one had turned the corner.

Anxiety

"Vince! Quick! I need to have a word with you!"

Natalie's loud whisper was more of a hiss as she beckoned Vince into the kitchen by waving a small sock at him.

Dennis, who was now aware of the recent promotion of Vince, was leaning over the bar discussing football results with Trevor. In the absence of any other lunchtime customers, Vince decided he wouldn't be missed, and so wandered into the kitchen to liase with the distraught Natalie.

"I daw know what to do!"

Natalie was talking in the tones of one who was not used to being dramatic, but had watched far too many soap-operas.

"He's determined to have this baby. We're at it round the clock. He was never like this, even when we first met!"

This was far too much information for Vince and had a similar effect on him as the smell of Malibu the day before.

Vince panicked and offered a compliment in reply.

"Well good on ya, Nat!"

"Good on ya! Is that all what you have to say, Vince! If I get pregnant in the next month it may very well not be good for either of us. I've no idea what happened on New Year, and quite clearly neither do you!"

Natalie's hissed whisper was louder than her normal talking voice and Vince looked over his shoulder to make sure Dennis hadn't wandered in.

"Yaw can't carry on working here, Vince. Yaw just can't. You'll have to tell him you've found another job somewhere."

Vince was surprised by the turn of events and took a moment to work out his blackmail options. He'd rather assumed that, as a washer-upper with little to lose, in the current situation he was actually the one that was better placed to issue demands. However, it was Natalie who was kicking him out, so this needed a re-think. Would she really tell Dennis about waking up with Vince? If Dennis found out by some other means, what was the worst that could happen? An initial assessment suggested that the risks for Natalie included divorce, loss of income, homelessness, and the potential need to DNA-test a kid on the off chance its creation was inspired by Malibu, rather than a very small sock. Vince then turned to consider the risks that the situation posed for him. Essentially this stretched to a kicking from Dennis if his stamina was up to it, and loss of a job that he'd only had for two days. So, on the face of it, Vince won. This meant that if any of them had the right, then Vince should be the one doing the black-mailing. He was about to point this out when it struck him. Much as he should be the one yielding all the power in the seedy world of The Carrot and Jam Kettle, he wasn't. Did that mean that in his logical analysis he'd missed something? He looked at Natalie again and scrutinised her expression. She was staring at him with the confidence of one who was very anxious but who was also basically in control. Vince knew he would have to quickly reassess, and picked up where he left off. If Natalie had a baby, and it was a Malibu baby, then this would be followed by divorce, loss of income, and homelessness. Still pretty bad for Natalie. And then the most feared word of any potential father-to-be in an unconventional situation popped into Vince's mind. 'Maintenance'. Whose name would Natalie give to the Child Support Agency? Who would be paying maintenance to raise young Malibu to keep him in the luxury that he and his mother were accustomed to? It was unlikely to be Dennis. If you were the owner of a pub like The Carrot and Jam Kettle, then a slightly bigoted attitude was part of the essential profile to assist the locals to put the world to rights. Paying maintenance for Malibu baby wasn't going to cut it as a suitable topic.

"Alright then, Nat. But you owe me. And you'll have to be my reference."

Natalie's face sank from it muscle-taught agitated expression to one of relief and mild surprise. She'd not thought through the blackmail scenario quite as far as the maintenance issue, and so hadn't believed that Vince would be going along with it.

"Vince, you're the best. I'll do you're reference no problem. I'll pop to the bar and get your money and you can leave out the back of the kitchen."

Vince thought that if it was drama and suspicion they were trying to avoid, this probably wasn't the best plan. However, Baby-Malibu's 'maintenance' was a pretty powerful motivation, so he did what he was told.

The date

The front room of Jenny's mother's house had a slightly green tinge, that gave it a rather unusual ambience. Jenny had gone to make coffee so Vince voluntarily tried to close the curtains, only to find that the runners were stuck. It continued to be a night of revelations. The first revelation was that Jenny seemed to be genuinely interested in him. The second was that people really did go back for coffee, and this wasn't just a Hollywood thing. If it was, it had since caught on in the real world of the Midlands anyway. His latest revelation was that Jenny's mother must be the infamous Mrs Garret that was such a frustration to his nan's minimalist existence. Vince was pondering the probability that Jenny's mum had most likely re-married at some stage. The absence of either a Mr or Mrs Garret in the house at the late hour of his coffee excursion suggested that another name change in the future was not out of the question either.

The date, up until this point, had been going very well. Vince had picked Jenny up around seven. They'd gone to see some mushy girly movie that Jenny needed to see. Part way through, Jenny had touched his knee and whispered something incomprehensible. Vince had taken this as a cue to take a risk and put an arm around her. The move hadn't been rejected. It was not followed by an embarrassing scene involving an emotionally charged rant from a slightly mental woman about the inappropriate action of a 'disgusting pervert'. Or, in turn, act as a cue for the other feminists in the auditorium to applaud and sneer. So a far better result than the last time that he'd tried that move in a cinema. After the movie they'd discussed the plot and the characters in a quiet corner of a nearby wine bar before taking the bus back to their neighbourhood. Arm in arm they'd bought some chips and, having arrived at Jenny's door step, they'd had a slightly vinegary snog before she invited Vince in for coffee. Substitute the chips for a restaurant and the bus for a sports car, and there were parallels between this course of events and the plot in the girly movie they had just watched. Vince was wondering if women actually made men sit through these awful films early on in a date to help steer the man in the right direction for the remainder of the evening.

As Vince stared out of the window at the icy cars parked in the road, Jenny returned to the emerald chamber with two mugs of instant coffee.

"How do you take it, Vince?"

The old Vince would have made a crude joke at this point, but the new one replied politely that the coffee smelled good, and accepted the mug without further requirements.

"Shall we drink in here, Vince, or go up to my room?"

Normally Vince would have panicked at this suggestion. It was after all Jenny Davis, whom he had salivated over at school as a spotty out-crowder. It was also a first date, and less than forty-eight hours after throwing an underwear-clad Natalie Sedgwick into her coffee table and vomiting from her lounge window. However, the alternative to ascending to Jenny's bedroom was to make out with Jenny Davis in a green-lit room that was on display to the neighbourhood at large, and was being held under particular scrutiny by his own grandmother. Jenny led the way upstairs.

Rejection

Vince rolled over in bed and smiled at Jenny. Shafts of light filtered from the pale winter sunrise through the patterned curtains and fell delicately on Jenny's face as she slept peacefully. She was beautiful. She may have been a bitch at school. He may well have been confused about her interest in him right now. However, there was no denying the beauty of that face. Vince gazed at her and mopped a small bubble of dribble from the corner of her mouth. Jenny slowly opened her sleepy eyes and smiled up at him.

"Morning, Handsome."

The words enveloped him like a warm blanket of belongingness.

"Mornin' Jen. D'you sleep well?"

Jenny just smiled back. The silence was agonising. Vince was no good at this kind of small talk. It was hard enough with a few beers inside, but in the cold de-tox of morning it was desperately painful.

"What time you got to get to work, Jen?"

It was not that Vince wanted her to leave. He just had nothing else to say.

"I'm not working 'til tomorrow, Vince. I have the luxury of a long lie-in. When have you got to get back to your bartending?"

"I haven't really got to get back at all, Jen. Natalie Sedgwick gave me the shove yesterday. Lucky really. This means we can both spend the morning in bed."

Jenny sat up like a bolt and pulled the sheets around her.

"What! You've been sacked!? Jesus! I'd have been better off with Danny Bridges. He might have a fetish for rubber ducks, but at least he works for a living."

Before the end of this tirade, Vince had worked out why Jenny wanted to be with him. It certainly wasn't because she had suddenly stopped being a vain bitch. He'd already got one and a half legs in his trousers and was looking for a shirt. It wasn't necessary for Jenny to throw him out, but she did anyway. The process seemed to help her vent her anger and it helped Vince with 'closure'. That was what he thought to himself as he left the green world of Mrs Garrets, and sauntered up the road a slightly wiser man. Of course, he also thought that the whole 'closure' thing was nonsense, but they'd been going on about it quite a bit in the film he'd seen with Jenny. In his mind he was still drawing parallels.

The end of trade-up number 1

A more astute, more sceptical Vince turned up the frosty street where he lived. He headed past the untrimmed shrub, and manoeuvred his key in the unenthusiastic lock. His warm breath appeared in the cold air, like the smoke from cigars that have been given out to celebrate a great success. The symbolism was not lost on Vince. He was still the kid who had been rubbish at sport, battled against a daily onslaught of acne, and suffered social ineptitude. But he had just bagged Jenny Davis, and escaped to tell the tale. This was the stuff of urban legends.

Vince pushed open the paint-peeling door of number 18 and stepped inside his nan's house. He was a much wiser man than he had been four days before. Alright, he was out of work for now, but things had at least got interesting for a while. Vince decided he liked interesting. Trade-up number one hadn't gone quite as he planned. In fact, the brevity of trade-up number one was quite disappointing. Also, the whole idea of trading-up was that you swapped what you had for something better. He had lost what he had, and would have to start again. However, he'd not lost it all. He had gained a new confidence and a vision of what could be possible.

Vince peered down the hallway, beyond the thread-bare brown carpet where his nan was seated in her usual position.

"Yaw-right there Nan?"

"It's all pissin' cookin-ry programmes, Vincent. What's the point when we've all got pissin' microwaves now? Whatever happened to Les Dennis?"

Vince tried to make the Les Dennis connection as he watched his nan reach over and whack the side of the TV with her hand as an expression of protest against terrestrial TV programming. The aging TV set promptly made a sharp hissing noise and the screen went blank.

"Pissin' hell!"

Chapter 2 – Brake cables

Cables

Roy Buckworth had the gait of an unperturbed heron, and the face of a disgruntled lizard. Surprisingly, this was a combination he shared with a number of his colleagues. His strut along the walkway between the machinery at the factory was crafted over time into an art work, depicting efficiency, menace and unwavering commitment. From the start of the line where the cables were stretched out, to where they were coated in plastic, cut to precise lengths, the ends were die-cast and they were tested and packed, nothing escaped Roy Buckworth. It wasn't as if people hadn't tried to get away with sneaking off for a crafty fag, or taking too long in the toilets. However, Roy had one major advantage over all of them. He enjoyed his work, whilst those beneath him had only the motivation to skive off theirs. Like the ultimate game of cat and mouse, the cat may have the occasional bad day or lapse in concentration, but the game only ends when the mouse loses. Roy loved being a cat. Or a lizard-faced heron, depending on which analogy you go for.

When studying Buckworth, Vince was torn between the two analogies. However, he had one of the world's most dull jobs and therefore had plenty of time to ponder over it. A wise man called Mike Ashbury, who was going through his third divorce and his fifth set of paperwork at the Child Support Agency, had once pointed out to Vince that it was no good getting a boring job. It may appear to be a good plan to be under-challenged and not stressed by your occupation, but unfortunately this gave you too much time to think about things. Thinking leads to regret, and regret leads to thoughts of the Child Support Agency. Vince was starting to appreciate the wisdom in this sentiment. With the machinery noise and his industrial health-and-safety ear-plugs in position, he couldn't even listen to music to deaden the monotony. At least the 'cat versus heron' debate of his internal monologue was taking his mind off the Natalie Sedgwick issue. This was a problem that was hanging-up in the back of his mind, like a slightly ripe carcass at the butchers that was past its mincing date.

It had been three weeks since Vince had visited the employment agency. He discovered that this method of job seeking differed from the normal job centre approach to losing your unemployment benefits in two key regards. Firstly, it was quite a fast way to get a job. Secondly the employer is paying the agency for finding them a steady flow of people to fill their mind-numbing jobs, and the agency then pays the employee as little as it can. Therefore, the remuneration for this quickly-found job was as low as it could possibly be whilst remaining legal.

Vince was an assistant to a bloke who had to die-cast aluminium fittings on to the end of brake cables for small European cars. To achieve his part in the double-act, he therefore pushed the cable into the hole of one machine so that the first inch of plastic was stripped. He then pushed the end into another hole that made the end into a bit of a lump for the aluminium to cling around. This was the job. No more, no less. Within two minutes he was quite proficient at his new career. Within ten minutes he even considered himself something of an expert. After three weeks of it, he was almost suicidal. He was certainly not convinced that this was a trade-up from bartender. However, Larry, the slightly eccentric die-caster to whom he was assistant, had told him that Roy Buckworth had called a team meeting. Within each eight-hour shift there were three ten-minute breaks. The meeting would be held after the second one at ten o'clock.

The ten minute break

For Vince, the ten-minute break at 9.50am involved trailing after Larry through a side door and spending eight and a half minutes in his company, along with a few other people who were, arguably, slightly more odd than Larry. The time, if managed properly, would allow for one and a half cheese sandwiches, half a bottle of coke, and two cigarettes. Cigarettes were an early form of Facebook from a simpler time before time-wasting went digital. Vince hadn't smoked since he was about seventeen, but in his efforts to fit in with the old school, the cigarette said 'I belong' in a way that his cheese sandwich would never achieve. Besides which, it offered a relatively eventful escape from being an assistant die-caster.

With his ear-plugs removed, Vince would learn who had got drunk the previous night, who had got very drunk and shagged their missus, and who had got even more drunk and shagged someone else's missus. One of the less vocal members of the group would then be ridiculed for not having been drunk enough to shag anything. It was a bit like being a speed bartender in a way. What would have been four hours of tedious non-gossip in the bar that had to be politely endured, was condensed down into a few minutes before the ear-plugs went back in. In some ways they were very lucky the break was so short. It was still the end of January and very cold. The time it took to get rugged up would probably be equivalent to the other half of a sandwich in the summer.

In this particular break, shagging took a back-seat, so to speak, and Larry held court on the topic of the meeting.

"Bloody Royston! Him an his bloody pointless meeting. Bloody complete waste of bloody time. Just brown-nosing to the bloody management."

Griffo, who cut the wire into lengths at the bit of the factory before the die-casting, then piped up in support.

"Yawm expected to meet ya quota though ain't ya. All them time-management studies them suits done with their little stop-watches last year. Now they want to distract us from the quotas with these meetings, Larry."

All of them nodded at the sage observation offered by Griffo, including Vince out of a sense of comradely and an effort to keep warm. Personally, anything that saved him from another second of pushing a thin cable through a hole, waiting for the machine to strip the plastic off the end and then take it out again, was to be encouraged. Vince took another drag on his cigarette and wondered why, with all the complicated machinery in this high-tech factory, they hadn't got a machine that did his bit of the process as well.

"Way hey, Vincy!"

Larry dropped his fag-end and let out an exclamation as the distant figure of a thin girl with cropped black hair and a nose piercing walked past the end of the factory in the distance.

"She's bloody up for it, Vincy. I've seen the way she bloody looks at you my son. If you've not hit that by the bloody weekend then we'll all know you're as bent as a bloody two-bob! You'll have to watch yer self. Them Russians are into some pretty crazy bloody stuff."

"Alright, yeah, Larry. Good point."

Vince had become used to Larry's latest obsession over the romantic possibilities between himself and the black-haired girl of non-native but unconfirmed origins. For some reason her job required her to pass their part of the factory somewhere between the second and third part of the shift. Larry was determined that she passed by the die-casting area out of an irrepressible lust to get a glimpse of young Vince. Vince was quite convinced that the poor girl had no choice to do so as part of her job. Once you've walked passed Larry loudly giving his opinion on the matter of romance and the physical requirements thereof, you wouldn't walk past him again unless you really had to.

Larry started to make a couple of obscene gestures for the others to laugh at. Vince was glad that the young lady in question was now out of ear-shot, and he got started on the half cheese sandwich as time was quickly running out.

The team meeting

The team gathered in a quiet part of the stock area and sat on some large wooden reels that were used for the cables. Vince was surprised to learn that their team was about ten people. He knew three or four by sight along with Griffo, as they were working on the brake cable production near to his part of the scheme. The others were all new to him, but he wasn't about to start making introductions. He knew well enough that the new-boy in a place like this did well to keep his head down. As they arranged their giant cotton reels into a circle, Roy Buckworth entered the forum, and having found his perch he peered for a long time at his clip-board through his thick glasses before starting.

"We've got a couple of things on the agenda for today. Firstly, has anyone got any comments or something to share with the group before we start?"

Griffo, who clearly came from a similar gene-pool to that of Vince's nan, decided to relieve the pressure that was building inside his head:

"We were thinking about the quotas that we measured. Y'know, the ones from last year. I still don't know what our quota is. It would be helpful for the work if we knew, don't ya think, Mr Buckworth?"

Roy Buckworth's response was both authoritative and patient, as he peered with his magnified eyes at the questioner.

"Sorry, William. I think we covered this at the last monthly meeting. The management did not do the time-study so that you could know what your quota is. It is only important that they know what your quota is."

Griffo nodded in agreement like he was part of some intellectual debate. Vince was starting to find himself in the unlikely category of being in agreement with Larry. This meeting was pointless.

"Next item. Current orders."

Roy Buckworth proceeded to refer to a list on his clip-board of current brake cable orders and then a long explanation of the degree of confidence the management had in finalising an order for Toyota brake cables. This was apparently of more interest to the others than it was to Vince. A couple of them asked questions afterwards. This was all good for Vince as it was eating away extra moments before he had to return to repetitive employment. Roy flipped over the paper on his clip-board to the last page.

"Finally on the agenda: team building. The management want you to feel more like you are part of the team. The plan is that if you have any good suggestions of how to improve our efficiency, or the way we work, then they want to hear your ideas. That way we can all build the team together and we might get more orders like the Toyota one."

The others nodded with interest. Vince could tell a scam when he heard one. If they came up with a good idea to improve efficiency then the management would benefit and the team would probably have to work harder. If they didn't come up with a good idea then the management would say that at least they'd tried to let them be part of the bigger picture and encourage them. If the team complained about something in the future then the management could say that they were given this opportunity but they didn't bother to take it. It was win-win for the management and lose-lose for them. However, as they'd not thought it through that far it seemed to cheer up the others in the team a bit, and Vince couldn't care either way. The very fact it had been on the agenda at all had delayed his return to his station, and for that he was grateful.

Roy wrapped up the meeting and they all trundled back to their jobs.

As he walked back, Vince passed the black haired, pierced, and allegedly Russian girl. He glanced at her with a slight look of embarrassment. To his surprise he could swear that he received the slightest of coy smiles in return. Maybe Larry was a better judge of the subtleties of human emotion than Vince had given him credit for after all.

Kaleena

Kaleena Pawlowski was a Polish national with a European passport. She had been groomed by her family so that when she was eighteen she would travel to England and spend her summer working on a fruit farm. She would toil for long hours at backbreaking work: crawling on her knees between damp rows of strawberries in the pre-dawn cold; tearing her arms to shreds as she plundered gooseberry bushes; feeling the strain on her back has she hauled sacks of apples back from the orchards. The aim was to make hard currency that she would then bring back to the fold and make everyone in the Pawlowski clan very proud. This is exactly what the Czerwinski family that lived on the opposite side of the street had been doing for years with their children, and they had a new Skoda. The Czerwinski's had even invested in producing two extra children to ensure the sustainable future of this fruit-based cash cow. Kaleena's mother, driven by greed and jealousy, has gone to the extent of sending Kaleena to work in Polish fruit farms for the past two summers to ensure her daughter was properly trained up for her international debut on the fruit scene.

Kaleena had arrived at a fruit farm in Herefordshire where she stayed with other Polish kids, mainly students, and spent long hours in the fields picking gooseberries, strawberries, beans, and eventually apples. Accommodation was provided in the form of a couple of old caravans where the students kept a low profile from the authorities and the farmer maintained his low profile from the tax office. Kaleena dutifully sent the money home to her mother who immediately bought a new dress and a leather coat so that she could parade down the street in them for the benefit of Mrs Czerwinski. However, Mrs. Pawlowski had failed to pick up on the full implications of her country joining the EU in recent years. This meant that the benefits of this scheme under the single-market system and the Euro were unlikely to add up to a new Skoda. It also meant that once Kaleena had fulfilled her destiny and boosted the family wealth, she was at liberty to stay on in the UK and find herself a job, as was her European constitutional right.

The fruit season was over and the caravan was cold, so Kaleena and a few others from the farm gravitated to the nearby towns. To the despairing workers at the town's employment centres these kids were the easy part of their day. The new Polish arrivals had low expectations, limited relevant skills, and a fairly poor grasp of the English language. Their low expectation was therefore what singled them out from most of the people that passed through the system, and so finding them work was relatively easy.

Since her recruitment at the factory, Kaleena had shared a small flat with two other Polish friends and had been working at the factory in the logistics department. This was mainly filing delivery and dispatch notes. The stock taking meant that she had to make checks in the stock area at the far end of the factory beyond the cable making line at least once a day. This is the task that brought her past the die-casters each morning. It was very much to her benefit that the English lessons which she'd received at school in Poland covered very little of the same vocabulary that Larry's education had provided him with.

The idea

An idea that is borne from apathy is rarely going to be a good one. However, combine this with Mike Ashbury's 'too much time to think' theory, and you might just have something.

It was the third time since Vince had started at the factory, that some technician from Birmingham had been brought in to mend the die-casting machine. For his part, Vince had completely filled up the shelf where cables waited to be die-cast and so had stopped doing any more. He assumed that if the management knew what the quota was, that they would also know it was different when the machines didn't work. It was while he had even less to fill his mind than usual that the ingenious idea popped in.

Since Roy Buckworth had requested ideas, Vince had been toying with the notion that he should probably suggest one. Of course it was all a scam, but if the idea got him noticed and led to some kind of promotion that allowed him to trade-up then it was worth it, if only to him. On many occasions he had previously wondered why they didn't make a machine which would carry out his own pathetic and automated job. However, his experience in the cable trade now included watching Larry deciding there was a die-casting problem and messing with the settings on his machine. If there really was a problem, then this fiddling presumably made things worse. Eventually, the situation would require Dave from Brum to make a special trip over and put things right again. The burning question was no longer whether or not to replace Vince with some kind of simple robot, or at least someone who would be intellectually stimulated by the task. The question was whether to replace Larry with someone who was actually fully trained, and replace the machine with one that worked. Replacing Brummy Dave with someone who could make the thing go for longer than a week without it breaking again would probably help a bit as well. It was as Vince thought through the logic of his tedious argument that his idea came to him.

"Toilet stop."

Vince shouted his immediate intentions at Larry so that he would have an alibi for his absence later on if necessary. Larry was too busy kneeling next to Brummy Dave showing interest in what he was doing. He was no doubt hoping that everyone on the line would leap to the conclusion that he was Dave's equal and contributing meaningfully to resolving the highly technical problem.

Vince wandered off towards the loos. Fortunately they were near to the offices where the workshop floor management sat and deliberated over the big brake cable issues of the day. Through the glass door, Vince could see that Roy Buckworth was sitting at his desk pouring intensely over some paperwork. His tentative knock failed to get Roy's attention so he opened the door and walked in. Roy looked up with a degree of annoyance. He did not appreciate interruptions.

"Vince isn't it? You want something? Make it quick though. Very busy."

Roy was using short sentences to give the implication that he was in a hurry when he probably wasn't. Vince made a mental note of this technique, in case it could come in useful for him in the future.

"Alright, Mr Buckworth. I was thinking about your asking for ideas the other day. I think I might have had one."

Roy Buckworth looked without interest towards Vince. The ideas thing was a management gimmick from the people on the second floor that they'd probably read about in some 'How to be a better manager' book. To Roy, it was nonsense to believe that the likes of Griffo or Larry could have an idea, good or otherwise. They did the jobs that they had because they were not at the cutting edge ideas-end of the work force.

"What's the idea then, Vince?"

"Out-sourcing, Mr Buckworth."

"Out-sourcing. Right then. I'll tell them upstairs and let you know."

"I think you should, Mr Buckworth. It'll probably save a lot of money. I imagine they'll promote you to the upstairs as well like."

Roy Buckworth hesitated. It was not something he did often. He was suspicious of all people. He trusted no one and looked out for only himself. He'd been around long enough to know those were the only rules worth following. To stray from those guiding principles was unadvisable. However, there was something about Vince. He didn't quite fit in. The way he clearly kept his head down at the meeting and around the factory wasn't natural, but to Roy who was a professional observer, he saw that it was calculated. Maybe this lad did have a bit more about him than the others.

"So, how does the 'out-sourcing' work?"

"For the bits of the process along the line that don't work well, you send the wire to another factory. Our die-casting is the end of the line but the machine is hopeless. It's always breaking, and no one here knows how to fix it. Why not send the cut cables in a transit to where Brummy Dave works to have the die-casting done there? If they've got a better, more reliable machine then it'll probably work out to be cheaper."

Roy Buckworth stared in both amazement and bafflement at what he had just heard. What he'd heard did make a lot of sense. However, he was being told this by the person who would lose his job if they carried it out. In which case, it made no sense at all. If it made no sense at all, then it was probably a bad idea.

"Wouldn't that put you out of a job though, Vince?"

"Change of job, Mr Buckworth. I could manage the shipping of the cables to the new factory. That or you'd find me something suitable once you made it to the second floor."

Roy Buckworth thought about it for a moment. Roy wasn't a bad person and so wouldn't steal the idea from Vince and present it as his own. However, he had to follow this through in a way that gave him a lot of the credit. Similarly he needed to make sure that if it back-fired he didn't take the fall either.

"I'm having a drink this evening with Ted Rositer and Darren Littleton at The Crown. It's pool night and we're in the quarters, along with one of Ted's buddies. Maybe you want to pop in and have a beer and a chat? About eight o'clock suit? We can think through this out-sourcing idea of yours in a bit more detail."

Beers with Ted and Dazzer then. Vince had absolutely no idea who they were. From the way they had been presented the assumption was that they were important people who would want to work with him on his out-sourcing idea. Worst case was that Roy just wanted to hear more in a place away from his colleagues. At least Roy would have to buy him a beer. Vince agreed.

He wandered back to the die-casting area, where Larry remained lying on his belly staring under the machine at what he could see of Brummy Dave on the other side.

"Back from a bit of reverse fishing then, Vincy!"

"Sommat like that, yeah."

The bus stop

Vince had originally thought that he would buy a bike and cycle to the factory. It was about three miles down the road from his house and there were no really big hills. It would also save money in the long run. However, there was nowhere to leave a bike at the factory, other than to chain it to the railings at the far end of the parking area that backed onto the railway cutting. It wouldn't be safe from theft, and would probably be subject to practical jokes from Larry. Also, arriving in a form of transport that was unlikely to either pull a girl, take a girl home, or be able to shag a girl in it, was likely to be the butt of a lot of jokes in the ten minute work breaks. The bus of course still failed to meet most of the above criteria from both a practical and legal perspective. Fortunately the bus stop was a little way along the road and so was unlikely that Larry would see Vince arrive and thus fail to be inspired to think all of this through.

Vince stood in the cold at the bus stop and looked at his watch. The bus was five minutes late. Minutes at a cold bus stop could be almost as long as minutes in the factory. He shuffled his feet to keep warm, and became aware that the black-haired, pierced foreign girl was standing near to him. Presumably if she had developed a good grasp of the culture and the transport system arrangements of her adopted country, then she was waiting for a bus as well. If not she was probably lost and requiring help. This would be unfortunate, as Vince didn't speak Russian. Otherwise she was simply there to be near Vince, as per Larry's theory of the daily factory walk-past. It was all very awkward. He should speak to her. Definitely. Earlier in the factory she had smiled coyly at him. It was done so subtly that it was almost un-spottable, and could easily be put down to either an over-active imagination or an under-active mind. Now she was standing next to him. She had laid the cards on the table. Now it was up to him to make his move.

Vince half looked at her. He didn't want to look at her full-on in case he'd been wrong about the coy look, and she would then think he was some kind of weird sexual predator. At the same time he didn't want to be not looking at her in case she thought he was just going to talk to himself. Having got himself at an angle which he decided was most appropriate, he knew it was time to throw caution to the wind and go for it.

"Yaw alright?"

There was then a very long pause which Vince considered filling with his own coy smile. He'd quickly realised that with his impetuousness and spontaneity he'd not thought this through at all. It was normally good to have at least one topic of conversation before starting a conversation. You could get away without having a topic when you started a conversation with your mates, but this did not work with a complete stranger.

"D'yaw take the bus then?"

The black-haired girl politely smiled at him before looking back up the road to see if the bus was coming. *Stupid question*, Vince thought to himself. *She's standing at the bus stop waiting for it*. It would help if he knew the Russian for bus. Vince decided to try a different tack. There was another long pause.

"I've seen you at work. Sometimes you come past our section. My name's Vince."

The girl turned to Vince and smiled again.

"Kaleena."

"That's an interesting name, Kaleena. Is it Russian or sommat?"

"I am a Polish."

"Arr, right."

Vince desperately tried to think of anything he knew about the Polish so as not to lose her attention now that the conversation was starting to flow more easily.

"You've got a lot of coal."

The puzzled face of Kaleena implied further explanation would be helpful.

"Well, not you. Your country. Poland. We did it in Geography like."

Kaleena smiled back and then pointed up the road.

"The bus, it is here. I going to town for shops. You want join? We have coffee?"

Vince followed her onto the bus and sat next to her. What was the modern world's (and particularly girls of dateable age) obsession with coffee? Surely *Friends* wasn't on in Poland as well?

The bus trip to town involved the continuation of a very stilted conversation carried out by two people with very little in common, which included their first languages. During their visit to the coffee house, however, things improved a little as Kaleena was able to teach Vince a little bit about the different coffee options on the menu. It seemed that Kaleena had worked in a restaurant that did posh coffee while she was finishing school. Vince had once been a bartender so finally, with serving drinks, there was something vaguely in common, and the embarrassing silences got slightly less painful.

Pool night at The Crown

Pool night, as with any competition whose competitors are passionate about their art, can be a very serious affair. In the case where the competitors are both passionate and a bit tanked-up, the seriousness can be far greater. Tuesday night down at The Crown was no exception. Roy and his mates had got there early for a swift pint and a quick practice before the lads from The Red Lion showed up. Roy, Ted and Darren had been in the pub league for six years now. Gavin had only joined last year as a bit of a hustler, as he was better than the rest put together. Ted Rositer worked in accounts and Darren Littleton was in the marketing department at the factory. It had started off as an excuse to meet up away from their wives for an after work beer, but had become something of an obsession over the years. This time, against all odds, they were in the quarter finals. Something they had only previously dreamed of.

Vince was not that interested in pool. The excitement of seeing a ball hit another one down a nearby hole was lost on him. At best it was a distraction for regular pub goers who had run out of conversation. He did, however, understand pool well enough not to point this out to those who were in to it.

Pool night was never going to be the ideal venue for Vince to make his pitch about his grand idea for out-sourcing. If anything was going to put it dead in the water, it was Vince talking shop at the time that Roy Buckworth's team failed to make it to the semis. This dilemma would still be the case, even if Roy's team won. A victory would mean that the conversation would deteriorate into a graphic discussion of every shot from each game. This was a conversation that could often fill an entire week; usually until the next round in the pool competition had started. It was no time to talk about changing a factory process by sending cables over to Brummy Dave's gaff.

It was partly for this reason that Vince had invited Kaleena to come along. They seemed to have bonded over coffee. They were two misfits from a factory that neither of them cared for, nor understood. Also, with her language limitations, Kaleena came across in Vince's world as marginally more socially inept than him, which was a good confidence booster. With Kaleena as his date, Roy would see that Vince was there in the pub, supporting in spirit, but not requiring to be accommodated socially. This need would have distracted Roy during the contest.

Vince actually quite liked Kaleena. She was attractive in a quirky sort of way, and was another step towards being back on track to rekindle the trade-up plan. According to his rules, each trade-up needed total commitment. Not just the work, but the girl, the car, and so on. A trade-up to a different girl was required along with the new lifestyle and the job. Bartending had been mildly successful in that regard. After all, despite the briefness of the trade-up, he had woken up with two different women. Admittedly this was only on one occasion with each woman, and in the first instance this was achieved with no memory of either how or why. Each trade-up should be a learning experience and therefore, with Kaleena, he planned to take things a little bit more slowly.

As he entered the bar, Vince could see through to the back room where the pool contest had just started. He shuffled round the bar with Kaleena in tow. Once he had caught Roy's eye and gave him a cheerful wave, he directed Kaleena to a corner table and then returned to the bar to get the drinks in. Kaleena had requested a pint of lager and Vince had been impressed. He returned to where Kaleena was patiently waiting. She smiled up at him as he put the drinks on the table. She was actually quite cute, even though she wasn't Russian.

Whilst he was at the bar he'd been planning the small talk and had not only returned armed with two drinks but arrived with a couple of uncomfortable-silence fillers as well.

"So, Kaleena. Why d'you get your nose pierced then?"

He decided that showing an interest in a girl's interests was always a safe bet, and decided to venture onto the subject of body art.

"Me and my small sister. We both get nose ring at same. I now look nose in mirror and think for my sister."

Vince decided this tale of impassioned sibling bonding across the continent probably sounded far more moving in the original Polish translation. It was pretty cool though.

"Have you got tattoos or anything like that?"

It was a fair guess. All the local girls he knew that had cropped, dyed black hair and a nose ring also supposedly had tattoos to match. Not that he'd ever been out with one.

Before she could answer, Roy Buckworth confidently strode up to the table, pool cue in one hand and a half empty pint glass in the other.

"Vince, glad you could make it."

"Alright, Mr Buckworth. How's the pool contest going over there?"

"Not bad, Vince. Not bad at all. I won my match, and Gavin has just won his. All we need now is for Dazzer to take the next one and we're through to the semis at The Black Horse next week. You should have seen me pot the black. Rebounded back into the top left without even touching the cush. Sweet."

Vince was seeing Roy in a new light as he beamed at the recollection of the ball going down the hole and his team shouting 'come on my son' for the benefit of the visitors from The Red Lion. At work, Roy was more like a miserable teacher doing playground duty on a cold day. On pool night, after a personal victory, he was the life and soul.

"Congratulations then. I won't get in the way of the game, Mr Buckworth. We can have a chat when it's all finished like."

Roy appreciated the gesture and called to the barman to pour another round of lager for his team, before he headed back towards the game with at least two springs in his step.

"Dragonfly."

"Wot?"

"I have dragonfly tattoo. But cannot show."

Kaleena tapped her lower left cheek and smiled. It was the same coy smile he thought he'd imagined in the factory. Vince enjoyed the way Kaleena rolled her 'r' as she said 'dragonfly'. It was like dating a Russian but without having to worry about relatives who could be in the mafia – which did seem to be the case in a lot of films. He was also grateful for both her sense of occasion and her coyness. After all, a display from his foreign date of an inappropriately located dragonfly was not going to be a good precursor for the 'out-sourcing' conversation.

"Why you need meet Roy Buckworths? He walk like pelican with illnesses."

Vince nodded in agreement. The cat versus heron debate had received a casting vote in favour of the humble pelican. He proceeded to tell Kaleena as best he could about his 'outsourcing' idea.

Kaleena was impressed. She had long since decided that the factory was very inefficient. She wondered why the employees at the factory tried so hard not to do any work. They had no pride in what they did, or in themselves. She therefore had no qualms with Larry no longer occupying his station on the route to the stock shed. Although she didn't entirely understand him, she was not unaware of the overall derogatory nature of the message Larry voiced each time she passed. Kaleena told Vince that she too had a plan for a brighter future. Once she had money she would to go to London to work in a hotel. She had been led to believe that so many Polish people did this it had reached the point that the hotel owners were surprised when applicants turned out not to be Polish. Some even gave out small bonuses on the Polish independence day.

The pitch

The pub had quietened a little and Vince and Kaleena sat with the factory pool team. It seemed that Dazzer had lost his match and so had Ted. This meant there would be a re-match at The Red Lion on Thursday. For Vince this was a pretty good result. The Crown team had not lost, and so were not too down-hearted. Meanwhile they wouldn't be too busy replaying the shots of their victory in their mind to ignore Vince.

Vince proceeded to explain his 'out-sourcing' idea in detail to the management. Ted was the first to react:

"That's an interesting way to look at things, Vince. A nice bit of 'lateral thinking'. How did you come up with that?"

"I'm an assistant to the die-caster. I prepare the end of the cable before it gets cast, so I've had plenty of time to see how things work down there."

"We'd need to do a study of the finances. Work out what the costs would be to ship the cables over to Pratt and Sons, how much they would charge for the services, and compare it to the current costs of that part of the factory. What d'you reckon, Daz?"

Dazzer was slightly less impassioned. He had just lost a pool match to Terrence Watson, a dodgy and slightly mouthy brick layer from the estate. Daz had been convinced that Watson had over-charged him for his extension and then not come and done the repairs when the window sills leaked the following autumn. Under such circumstances his under-enthusiasm was to be expected.

"The management might go for it. Depends how much they save and whether the clients will go for it. If we start out-sourcing to Pratt and Sons they might just take all their business there. I'll have a chat to a couple of people and see how they think the management will react."

Roy nodded thoughtfully. This was still a win-win for him. Management had asked for ideas, and they had one that Ted was prepared to do the financial analysis for. This made Roy the kind of go getter they needed on the second floor, regardless of whether the suggestion was accepted or not.

"Well done, Vince. It seems like we can take this forward to the next step. Good job. Looks like we're lucky to have you on the team."

"Thanks, Mr Buckworth."

Vince beamed back at his new middle-management buddies. The trade-up was going well.

Feedback

For the next few weeks Vince continued to spend his ten minute breaks with Larry and the crew. He was seeing Kaleena most nights but decided it was better to keep this low key. It was bad enough that she had to endure the barrage of comments as she walked past their die-casting station during working time. Adding on an extra ten minutes of Larry's jeering every two hours seemed unnecessary. Besides, Vince didn't want Kaleena to associate their relationship with time spent suffering Larry's displays of verbal dexterity. There was potential for a whole 'Pavlov's dog – conditioned reflex' thing, where the sight of Vince could make Kaleena's stomach turn due to the association with Larry's abuse.

Roy and Vince had crossed paths a few times and greeted each other cheerfully but briefly. Vince didn't want the others catching on that he was becoming chummy with the middle-management. Once you were on the shop floor you were required to wear your chip proudly on your shoulder and worship the god of inverted snobbery. 'Mates with Roy' wasn't a display that fitted with keeping your head down. Similarly, Roy was happy with the caste system in the factory as it helped him maintain his authority.

However, it was 9.55am on a Tuesday morning. There was time for one more cheese sandwich before the monthly meeting.

"Bloody Royston! Him an his bloody pointless meeting. Bloody complete waste of bloody time. Just brown-nosing to the bloody management."

"And we still don't know about our quotas, Larry. What was the point in all them time-management studies them suits done with their stop-watches last year."

Vince felt that he had stood in the cold through this conversation before. Monotony was apparently the key to life at the factory. They filed in and found some cable reels to sit on in the stock area. Vince watched the fork-lift guy whizz down one of the alleyways to fetch some boxes. It struck him that it was probably the most interesting job there, and if they did away with the die-casting he might ask if he could drive one of those instead.

Roy stalked up to the group and sat on a cable reel.

"Now, we've got a few things to get though on the agenda today. Firstly, are there any comments or something to share with the group before we get going?"

"I was wondering what our quotas were. We've not been told what our quotas are since the time-study was done last year, Mr Buckworth?

Roy patiently responded to Griffo's pointless question. Vince was starting to be impressed by Roy Buckworth. To go through this every time and not go mad was quite an achievement.

"Next up, we have some very exciting news."

Roy beamed in the direction of Vince with the same beam he'd used after winning his game of pool.

"The management has decided that we are going to buy a new die-casting machine!"

Some looked stunned, some cheered, Griffo clapped. They all then looked to Larry:

"That's bloody great news, Mr Buckworth. Thank you. You can thank the management from us as well."

Vince was always surprised how Larry would put on his act of loyal subservience for Roy Buckworth and yet slag him off behind is back at every other possible opportunity. It just made him look a bit ridiculous.

"Well, you can thank young Vince here. He's the one who got them thinking."

They all turned to look at Vince who was staring at the floor. Keeping his head down was an instinctive action at the factory but having heard Roy's bombshell, his neck was at a more acute angle than usual. Roy began to address Vince:

"We looked into the 'out-sourcing' thing and Ted Rositer spoke to Brummy Dave's mob and got some quotes for transport. The profit increase was there but it was marginal. Anyway, we spoke to the board and they decided that it wouldn't look good to the clients so they have decided that we will get in a new machine instead."

Vince looked horrified. He felt terrified. Not that the sums didn't add up or that the board had rejected it, but that this betrayal was being explained to an audience of Larry and his cronies. Larry then spoke:

"Well, bloody well done, Vincy! A new die-caster lads. I knew that boy had got something about him! Give him a cheer!"

Vince couldn't believe his luck. Larry had failed to pay enough attention to Roy to realise what had happened. He'd heard the phrase 'new die-casting machine' and then apparently his brain had switched off.

Roy continued down his list of notes on the clip-board. His grin seemed to get even bigger.

"The other news is that I will be moving up-stairs next week to the second floor. Brice Chester will be the new foreman until a replacement is recruited.

Eloping

As Vince returned to cable stripping, Mike Ashbury's 'too much time to think about things' philosophy was never more poignant. Vince's conclusion was clear enough. This trade-up had run its course. He may have got away with his deception in the meeting, but Larry wasn't that stupid. The inevitable penny of truth would drop sooner rather than later.

In the final break of the shift, Vince wandered round the side of the factory to look for Kaleena.

"Way-hey Griffo! Vincey's off to slip his Russian bird a quick one at the back of the car park."

Vince didn't react to Larry. It would just encourage him. Also, he didn't want to distract him from his dreams about the new die-caster so that he might examine the chain of events that led to its purchase. Kaleena was near a side door at the back of the factory having a smoke with what looked like the female version of Larry's gang. A bleached-blonde woman with too much foundation spotted him coming.

"Look out Sally! Some pervert's come to stare at us. What d'you want pervert. You come to stare at what you can't have?"

It really was the female version of Larry's gang. Fortunately Kaleena was already on her way over to him, and they continued around a corner and out of sight.

"How much money do we need to go to London?"

"London?"

"You said you were saving to go to London. Work in the big hotels with the other Polish girls. How much money do we need to do it?"

"The train to London, it is thirty-four pounds and sixty."

Vince was a bit surprised by this. He knew his pay was bad. How much worse was hers if she couldn't manage to save thirty-five quid?

"I'll buy your ticket then. Let's go tomorrow."

Kaleena thought about this. She liked Vince. She wanted to go to London. She didn't like the factory. She didn't enjoy break-time with Kaz and Sally.

"It is okay. I pack, but need to give rent to house-friend before go."

"Let's go now then!"

Vince would do anything not to go back inside the factory. He'd been paid last Friday so he would only miss out on a day and a half worth of pittance if he made a run for it now. Kaleena wrapped her arms around him and kissed him. She'd always dreamed of life where you threw caution to the wind, like some Roma adventure, and didn't have to be trained as a professional fruit-picker to impress Mrs Czerwinski. Holding hands they walked out of the factory gates and never looked back.

The call

Vince hadn't been looking forward to the call. When he had last been at The Carrot and Jam Kettle, Natalie had promised him a reference. It was now time to collect on that promise. The phone was in the kitchen, and so any call made in that house required competing against both the television and his nan's train of thought. His ever-present nan watched from her position by the electric fire as he lifted the receiver and he began to dial.

"That thing's not worth the pissin' line rental, Vincent. I just get calls from salesmen with their pissin' time-share nonsense."

Vince's nan gestured towards the replacement second-hand TV. She had sourced it via a classified ad in one of the free-papers that collected as an ever-building fire hazard beneath the front door.

"That's the woman that's been fitted with one of them elastic bands they put around your stomach. Costs a pissin' fortune they say. She should just get off her pissin' backside and walk to the shops each day like the rest of us. Mrs Garret was at the grocers yesterday and says they've changed the shop around so that the papers are now in the middle, and you've got to go all the way to the pissin' back to get the tinned fruit."

Vince was glad to hear Natalie's voice on the other end of the phone. Much as he had been dreading the conversation, he really didn't want to have to think about day-time TV presenters having elective surgery on their digestive systems, or even Mrs Garret's tinned-fruit dilemma. If Dennis Sedgwick had answered the phone it would have been more awkward, and Vince had yet again failed to prepare a back-up conversation for that eventuality. He doubted that Dennis would appreciate a call where a panicking ex-employee invited him to offer an opinion on surgically inserted elastic bands.

"The Carrot and Jam Kettle, Natalie Sedgwick speaking."

"Alright Natalie. It's Vince."

Natalie's voice with its contrived, chirpy, singing call-centre tone deteriorated rapidly to her usual Midlands drone.

"What d'you want, Vince. I thought we agreed you were going to keep away? Dennis still doesn't know why you left and I've no bloomin' intention of letting him find out."

"It's all right, Nat. I'm not looking for trouble. I just need that reference. The one you promised. I'm going to look for work in the hotel trade so I need you to say that I've got experience in the catering and hospitality trades."

"They reckon you're closer to a rat when you're in a hotel than when you're in a pissin' sewer these days."

"Nan! Shush! Sorry, Nat."

"Dennis is going down to the Cash and Carry this afternoon. We're getting low on vermouth and the box of scratchings finished on Sunday. Come round about four-thirty and I'll have it ready. Come to the kitchen door."

"Thanks Nat."

"They're in the walls you see. There was a big one in the rubbish last week before the bin-men came. I had to throw a pissin' saucepan at it. I reckon they're coming over the wall from Mrs. Barry's Their bins are always full of pissin' take-outs from the Indian."

Vince returned the receiver to the hook. He really needed to think about getting a mobile phone as part of the next trade-up. And besides, why was his nan going through Mrs Barry's rubbish bin?

The reference

Vince glanced around the pub car park and noted that Dennis's red Volvo was absent and no doubt engaged in the vermouth run. He wandered across to the building and knocked on the kitchen door. He'd never done that before. Normally he just wandered in, put on an apron and started chiselling at the scorched remnants of what had been welded to the grill the night before. Natalie opened the door.

"Come on in, Vince."

Her voice was softer than on the phone. With Dennis out of the way she was less anxious.

"How you bin? I'm sorry how things worked out."

Vince was surprised. He was waiting for a conflict that never came. He glanced at Natalie's mid-rift. There was no sign of a bump, not that there would be, as it was only the third week of February. If Natalie had noticed him look she didn't respond. She was used to people in the bar admiring her figure and dressed to encourage it. She was probably immune to a more subtle peer.

"I've put in a bit about hospitality, and how you assisted with the catering and the bar. You'd better read it and make sure it's okay."

Vince read through the reference. It wasn't bad.

"Thanks Nat. I'm so sorry I can't remember what happened that night. I didn't mean for it to end up like this. I enjoyed working with you."

"Well, it was me that got us both drunk, and Dennis who sent me down that road in the first place. Let just blame him, eh."

Natalie kissed Vince on the cheek and gave him a hug.

"Good luck in the big smoke city."

"Thanks Nat. Good luck to you too."

Vince left The Carrot and Jam Kettle with a degree of confusion. Maybe Natalie still held a flame for him. He had hoped to make a clean break but instead was leaving a trail of unfinished business. The sooner he got out of town the better.

8.33 to London

The station that served the suburban sprawl was like any other. Weeds grew at the base of the opposite platform, despite the trains shunting past and coating them in a thick layer of black pollution. Weeds grew even more vigorously beyond the sign at the end of the platform that challenged you not to venture further. Amateurish graffiti coloured the back railings and the concrete pillars that supported the iron bridge that led across the tracks. Presumably it was a practice area for the more elaborate designs on the signal box further down the line. For Vince, this uninspiring, grey, wound-like laceration within a greyer town added to his motivation to move away. Who could stand here waiting for a train while holding a one-way ticket and find any reason to change their mind. Strictly speaking he had two one way tickets as he had bought Kaleena's. However, the principle remained.

Kaleena came through the small station, past the ticket office, and joined him on the platform with a quick hug. She beamed at him as she dropped her small pink suitcase on the platform next to him, and then disentangled herself from the enormous pink suitcase her mother had given her before leaving Poland. Presumably its purpose was to buy luxury western items to bring back and flaunt for Mrs Czerwinski.

"I am excited to be going London. It like movie from Poland. Bakery man has son who go with country girl to Warsaw to start bakery. This is exact same."

Vince smiled at her and held her hand. She was right. This was a real adventure into the unknown, albeit devoid of a bakery theme. It was certainly the most adventurous thing he had ever done in his life. He'd been on a school trip to Brittany once when he was eleven, but that was about it. He was very glad that Kaleena was there.

"The train's coming now."

Regional trains were fairly uninspiring ways to start auspicious journeys. They were neither pointy, fast or exotic. They usually looked like three carriages stuck together with a small room on the front for the driver, with a door in the middle in case it needed to become just a carriage again. However, it fitted with the ambience of the station, and the desire to spend little time on a train like this gave another reason not to have a change of heart and return part way into the journey.

Kaleena hit the button at the side of the door to make it hiss open and Vince loaded both of their bags into the space at the back of the carriage.

He sat next to Kaleena and looked out of the window.

"It's bye-bye to all of this then. It's like a monkey-puzzle tree. The only thing to do if you start climbing is to keep going up. There's no turning around. If you're a monkey that is."

"Why you think I monkey. It is my toes that are long?"

Chapter 3 – Hotel

Reception

"Your key, Sir? Room 3-0-4 was it? Very good, Sir. Breakfast will be served from a quarter past six until nine-thirty in the dining area. Enjoy your evening, Sir."

Vince had always prided himself on his ability to do a good Michael Caine impression. However, he had never imagined it would be of any practical use. Indeed it had even failed in the realms of impractical use up until now. Despite this, remarkably his English accent was a key talent leading to his success when interviewing with the owner of the cheap Paddington hotel where he was currently the receptionist. The majority of workers in the service trade in cheap London hotels were Eastern European with a limited grasp of the local dialect. Few nationals tended to be drawn to the low pay, unsociable hours and the lack of security offered by the informal sector. However, he was a Midlander with limited options and a CV highlighting a brief stint contributing, in a limited way, to part of a brake cable. Work in a cheap hotel was therefore something of an opportunity.

Through Kaleena's network of Polish friends they had got interviews at a hotel near to Paddington station. The owner, Susan Ratcliffe, had seen great possibility in both of them. As far as Kaleena was concerned, Susan Ratcliffe had had good experience with the Polish girls that had passed through, as they worked hard and accepted the low pay. As for Vince, not only did he have a good command of the local language but he was also the right size for the vacant receptionist's uniform. His accent was a little odd, but the American tourists that stayed for a couple of days before taking a coach trip to Stratford would lap it up. Other guests were usually people from the north. They were often down for just one or two nights whilst staying in the capital for a specific event like a concert. That or they were staying there on their way to Heathrow airport. Either way they wouldn't care or notice the way that Vince talked. Also, as Vince and Kaleena were a couple then they could share one of the rooms that needed refurbishing on the top floor on the east side of the building, and the rent could be deducted from their pay.

Vince had decided that the reception job was a bit similar to bartending. You worked behind a small bar-like desk. You greeted customers and dealt with their needs, like a room or a key. You also arranged their bill and took the money. However, unlike bartending, you rarely had to listen to nonsensical drunken conversations with the air of one who cared. Similarly, you didn't have people ordering obscure drinks you'd never heard of. It was definitely a good trade-up and things were back on track. It wouldn't be long before Vince became someone worth being.

Kaleena was also happy with her work. As a young girl she had dreamed of travelling beyond the confines of small Polish town life. She would go misty-eyed at the thought of visiting the big cities of the world, the seven wonders and even the Polski Fiat factory in Warsaw. Her childhood fantasy was not hunting for strawberries in the cold of the early morning whilst crawling along on her knees in muddy straw, nor indeed spending her valuable days in a dusty Midlands factory, receiving verbal abuse from bored co-workers. The hotel work was of course menial. However, it was an environment in which politeness was favoured and vulgarity was not directly correlated as a measure of status.

Paddington

In addition to being a stop off for tourists heading north, or northerners heading south, Paddington was also where you stayed if you wanted to be close to the London tourist attractions, but were prepared to exchange an extra twenty minutes of travel to get to them for a lower hotel bill. It was also convenient for Heathrow airport as you could get a regular underground train to the terminals. The alternative was to stay at airport hotels which were similar in price, had expensive bars and restaurants full of people on their way to Ibiza or Crete, and required buses to get to and from the terminals. The option of a Paddington stop over was therefore competitive as there were plenty of cheaper places to eat.

Vince had settled well into his new role. He was good at the job and had received no complaints from either his superiors or the guests. The hours were a bit odd, but he was used to that from both the pub work and the factory shifts. He was in a new exciting town, with a job and a girlfriend.

In the few weeks that they had been there, they'd spend their time off visiting a number of the main attractions. Kaleena had a list that needed ticking off, which included the Tower Of London and Madame Tussauds. It was a very happy time. Vince took photos of her outside each attraction. This was so they could be sent back to Poland and shared by her mother with Mrs Czerwinski as continued ammunition for the on-going rivalry. They also had to do a lot of shopping for her mother. The brief had been to find items that were not available in Poland so that Mrs Pawlowski's home would become a showroom of the exotic. However, there wasn't much in London that you couldn't get in the rest of Europe these days. As a result, Kaleena's stock of showroom items was an assortment of tea-towels with scenes of London, jars of jam with traditional English landscapes on the labels, and a number of large slippers made in the shape of stuffed animals.

Were it not that Kaleena's job included changing the beds and cleaning the toilets of drunken tourists who were looking for the cheapest accommodation in London, then it would have been even better.

Despite the work, Kaleena was comfortable with her decisions. Leaving the factory for London had been the right choice. Leaving for London with Vince had also been the right thing to do. Somehow he was different to other boys she knew. He seemed to exude ambition, and be willing to take risks. Also he was kind to her, which had not always been the case in her past relationships. Her friends had put her in touch with a few Polish people they knew in London that lived a few tube-stops over in an area called Whitechapel. Vince and Kaleena had been to visit there a few times on the tube. It was nice for Kaleena to get to talk Polish again. However, the guys in Whitechapel seemed to have an agenda. A bit like her, they were only in the UK to make money. It had helped to reminder herself why she enjoyed being with Vince so much. He seemed to be driven by a different ambition. The money would never be the key issue for him. He wanted to be content with all aspects of his life.

Responsibility

Vince had been working at the hotel desk for about a month when the manager, Mr Warwick Masterton, decided that Vince was ready for a bit more responsibility and called him into the office:

"Morning Vincent! Have a seat."

Masterton gestured to the delicate-looking wooden chair at the side of his small desk. All the rooms in the hotel were fairly small. The hotel was a series of three tall, thin, aging townhouses that had been connected together by a corridor on the ground floor. Subsequently all of the rooms, including Masterton's office, were thin and aging, and the choice of appropriate furniture needed to take this into account.

"I'll be heading off for about week, I'm afraid. I have a funeral to attend in Peterborough. This means that from this afternoon you'll have to be in charge."

This was not something Vince had been expecting at all. Not only had he never considered taking on a position of responsibility like that, no one had ever considered him as responsible before. The notion, therefore, came as a bit of a surprise.

"I see, Mr Masterton."

"Yes, it's all rather unfortunate timing. Of course Mrs Ratcliffe is off on some cruise in the Caribbean at the moment so there's no way she can pop in and cover for me."

"What d'yaw want me to do like?"

Vince didn't bother doing his Michael Caine voice for Masterton. Vince had interviewed in his normal voice and it was Masterton who had encouraged him to put on something a bit posher for the benefit of the American guests. Vince also suspected that Masterton was a bit dodgy himself. For example, Vince greatly doubted that a funeral in Peterborough was the genuine reason for Masterton's sudden departure. However, the cause of Masterton leaving the hotel was far less of a concern than the consequence of Vince becoming in charge.

"In addition to the reception work I'll put you in charge of the petty cash. This means you have to pay the suppliers for the food delivery to the kitchens and cover any additional needs down there. You will need to monitor that the kitchen and cleaning staff are at work and doing their jobs. You also have to change the shifts around in case there is a need to find cover. I'll give you my mobile number in case of an emergency."

Masterton then spent twenty minutes talking Vince through the shifts and how the rotas worked. He then talked through the expected deliveries. Finally he showed him the safe for the petty cash and demonstrated how to open it using the code. They then went to the kitchen to look at the stocks and talk more about the deliveries before returning to Masterton's office.

"Now Vincent, you have my number and the master-keys. Do you have any questions at all?"

"Not really, Mr Masterton. I've got yaw number to call just in case, like."

"Very good. Mrs Ratcliffe will be back from her cruise next Friday. I've sent her a message, so she knows I'm away and that you are covering. I'm sure she'll be in on Saturday to check on you. I'll be back on the Sunday. I'm sure you'll be fine and I'll make sure you get a decent bonus for this at the end."

With that, Masterton shook hands with Vince, grabbed his coat that was draped on the small bookcase in the corner of the room and headed out of the hotel.

Susan Ratcliffe

Susan Ratcliffe was the owner of the Armstrong Hotel, Paddington. It was originally her husband's business and named after George Armstrong Custer, famed for his last stand at Little Bighorn. Alan Ratcliffe had originally wanted to call it the 'Custer Hotel' but his friends had guided him away from this idea, pointing out that it might get mistaken as the 'Custard Hotel'. This was a name which didn't sound very classy, and was perhaps more suitable for a toddler day-care centre. When Susan had wedded him she was a little put-out to discover that when she had married into the hotel trade she had not only acquired access to his substantial money, but also to his kitchens.

To motivate his new and disgruntled bride, Alan Ratcliffe had tried to expand the dining area into a proper restaurant for both guests and customers. It was the eighties. Bad decisions were the norm, and not only had Alan married a woman with a white handbag and blonde perm that was so full of hairspray it crunched when you touched it, he also ended up with a restaurant selling nouvelle cuisine. This was a very eighties thing to do. However, so was spending a fortune on a mobile phone which could also double as a house brick. A cheap hotel on an inconspicuous street near to Paddington Station was never going to attract the decadent hoi polloi that the restaurant needed to justify its small portions of expensive and decorative food. In the 90's they regrouped and developed a couscous-based menu for their clientele, bringing a Lebanese flavour to the cuisine. However, for some reason, this also failed to take off.

By the time of the Lebanese cuisine disaster, Susan and Alan had become quite distant. The marriage became a façade to help the tourists to believe they were staying in a respectable family-run establishment. Alan had been involved in an affair with one of the cleaning staff, whom Susan had subsequently sacked. Since then he had been having an on-off affair with the female train guard on the London to Carlisle route, which meant his mistress was only in town on Tuesdays, Thursdays and Sundays. He had met her whilst taking the train to Knutsford in

Cheshire to join his colleagues of the American Combat Re-enactment Society, to take part in a weekend-long recreation of the 'Battle of Greasy Grass'.

As their relationship grew, his mistress, for whom part of the appeal of her occupation had been the uniform, later signed up to the society as a private in the 7th Cavalry. Susan, meanwhile, had taken to going on expensive cruises every few months and having short steamy affairs with anyone in a sailor uniform. She had reached the stage where she actually packed extra sailor uniforms for any eligible men on the boat that she liked the look of but had failed to pursue a nautical career.

The restaurant returned to what the customers had always wanted: a provider of English breakfasts for the tourists, which was served with English breakfast tea. A slight misnomer, considering tea is not produced in England. However, this always failed to discourage the enthusiasm of confident brash American tourists who loudly discussed the matter of eating 'traditional English fare' for the benefit of everyone else in the dining area. They were unaware that an unwilling audience failed to be impressed at their loud opinions overpowering their own early morning inner-monologues, with which they and their hangovers were already quite content.

Susan Ratcliffe was not a generous woman, and had perfected the fine art of appearing to provide a hearty fry-up breakfast at the lowest cost. This extended to ensuring that the cheapest ingredients were prepared and served by the smallest number of poorly paid staff. Once this was achieved, there was little for her do other than the occasional spot-check in-between cruises. In the mid-nineties Alan had died of a heart-attack shortly after a re-enactment of the battle of Little Bighorn. This was widely put down to a combination of the fiery passion that the irregularity of seeing a train-guard from Carlisle can induce, and the fact that he regularly ate the oil-soaked breakfasts that his hotel churned out each morning. No association was ever drawn to the fact that he had spent his weekend fannying about on a horse pretending to be shot at by Sioux Indians in the middle of Gloucestershire. In the absence of Alan, Susan immediately hired a string of managers to oversee the daily running of the hotel. The latest was a man called Warwick Masterton. He was quite a dodgy character and she immediately assumed that this was not his real name. However, he presumably was desperate enough about something in his recent past not to use his own name, and therefore would be cheap. Also, he would probably have fewer scruples about the out-of date meat they used for the sausages and bacon.

Management

Vince had never been 'management' before and decided to make the most of it. There was little that could go wrong in the space of a week. Masterton's office was next to reception and so Vince was aware that Masterton actually didn't do a lot of work. It was more that he was there to balance the books and make decisions for Susan Ratcliffe. The staff all knew how to do their jobs. The cleaners were always ready to start on time as they were not paid hourly and so were happy to get their work over with as quickly as they could. Also, these same cleaners worked as waitresses during breakfast as well, which finished at the same time that cleaning started. The cook was also well-rutted into his routine and had been churning out greasy-spoon cuisine at the Armstrong Hotel for more than ten years.

Kaleena was impressed.

"We should go for celebration. Big meal. Maybe steak. Maybe we eating falafel."

Since her arrival in Paddington, Kaleena had been through a number of fads. It started with humus from the Greek café near the underground, this had subsided following her discovery of chicken satay, and most recently she had fallen for Yemeni falafels. It was certainly broadening Vince's horizons beyond his diet of fish and chips, where the option of curry sauce is the main passageway offered into the world of gastronomy.

Late nights were not on the cards these days as Kaleena's six day week included a 6.15am start in the kitchens. Vince usually worked from 7.00am in the morning until 12.30pm, and then from 2.30pm to 8.00pm. A retired Indian guy, named Anil, came and sat behind the desk at night where he watched a small black and white TV until he fell asleep. Kaleena often turned the TV off on her way to the breakfast shift and prodded Anil so he'd look awake if Warwick or Susan arrived early. A student called Dan from the Royal College of Radiologists worked reception on Sundays.

As soon as Anil turned up for his Friday night sitcoms and snooze, Kaleena and Vince hit the streets of Paddington. Falafel won the day and there was a slap-up meal at the Yemeni restaurant. To make the celebration even more decadent they splurged on a couple of starters, and to her delight Kaleena learned that the Yemenis did humus as well.

Vince was enjoying being with Kaleena. She was nice to him, and fun to be with in an innocent sort of way. She did not need to be impressed with grand gestures. Simply learning about a new type of food was sufficient to keep her entertained for days. It was therefore a concern to him that he would eventually end up hurting her. She was part of a three-month trade-up, which had started when they'd first headed for London. They had been together for well over a month. This meant that it was time that he started thinking about the next trade. He had two months to turn his hotel receptionist position into something better. The fact that he'd been given this chance at responsibility from Masterton could be a real selling point. He could ask Masterton to be his reference and try for an assistant manager job in a bigger hotel. He should be looking at other options as well. The reason he was in London was the trade-up, and so he would have to trade all aspects of his life, which included Kaleena. Arguably Kaleena had already stretched over two trade-ups, having been part of his life when he was working in the factory and now they were together at the hotel. This was already something of a deviation from the rules. Vince started to question if he was tough enough to follow through with the trade-up scheme. It was easy enough to be motivated to progress when he thought back to his former life of scraping congealed slime from the back of the sinks at The Carrot and Jam Kettle. However, moving up the ladder would mean hurting people he cared for. The advantage of being a bottom-feeder on the food chain of success was that you never had to make selfish decisions or let anyone down. You just got to whinge about how other people did that to you. The tough side of trading-up was starting to hit home.

The Scam

An unusual element of the Armstrong hotel was that certain guests would come to the hotel, maybe once every two weeks, and ask specifically for Warwick Masterton. Vince would politely fetch Warwick from his office. After which Vince would be given some random task like rearranging the left luggage room or checking the light bulbs on the third floor. Warwick would then handle the registration and room booking personally. Vince would return to find that they'd long since been checked in and gone to their rooms, and that Warwick had returned to his office.

Vince at first had assumed that Warwick was sorting out a couple of friends with free accommodation on the sly. However, when Vince returned to reception, Warwick had always filled in the books, and their names and details were there on the ledger. They always left the following day and always paid their bill in cash. So, this left Vince assuming that these guys were just personal friends and to be attended to by their chum, Warwick. Had Vince been the one to serve these people he might have noticed that the faces of these loyal regulars didn't actually match with their ID. Their stolen identity was that of a citizen of similar age, height and colouring. These were picked from archived photocopies of one-time Armstrong Hotel guests, who had made short one-off visits. Warwick reproduced and copied these fake details from the files each time his friends came to visit.

This process had a number of outcomes. Firstly it meant that the hotel books added up, should anyone in authority start making enquiries. It would not raise questions at the tax office. If the phony guests were found out, at worst the hotel could be accused of being fooled by the false identity document. The IDs that were re-filed were mainly photocopies of driving licences, and so a blurred small photo made for a good excuse. Warwick was covered. Meanwhile there was no record of the gentlemen in question being at the hotel. As the Armstrong Hotel was a low market hostelry, Susan Ratcliffe had long since been persuaded by Warwick not to install security cameras. He had pointed out that the less opportunity for evidence to exist about their corner cutting in the restaurant supplies and various other health and safety measures, the better.

Before departing for some distant metropolis after their visits, the gentlemen friends of Warwick would give one of their debit cards to their wives to go shopping with, on the condition that they used the card in an ATM and then paid in cash. This meant that there was electronic evidence that they were in another part of the country altogether, and gave them an alibi. The result was that the Armstrong Hotel presented an environment of anonymity where they could conduct their business. In turn, the two gentlemen would present Masterton with an envelope of cash each time they stayed.

It was unfortunate that Warwick had failed to recall that his two friends were due to return on the weekend that he had left Vince in charge.

Warwick Masterton

'Warwick Masterton' was not his real name. It did have a ring to it though. Before becoming hotel manager, Warwick had been a bit of a wheeler and dealer in Birmingham. This had sometimes been fruitful but it also occasionally meant ripping people off with either faulty or stolen goods. At one stage he had sold a job-lot of televisions to someone he shouldn't have, which had caught the unfortunate attention of the police. The recipient did not appreciate the attention they had also received from the authorities and demanded compensation from their supplier. To address this he had borrowed money from other dodgy people that he couldn't afford to pay back. Effectively bankrupt, he had got on a train and headed south.

During the journey he had developed a number of false names to use when seeking new employment and opportunities. A combination of stress and a lack of imagination meant that most of these names were largely based on the stations he'd passed through on the way to London. These included Warwick Masterton, Stefano Leamington, Jules Banbury, and Michael Didcot. Jules Banbury had failed at an interview with an art gallery, Michael Didcot had successfully worked in a music store for a while and Warwick Masterton eventually struck gold in the hotel business. Despite a number of applications to the postal service and the *National Geographic*, the CV of Stefano Leamington had so far failed to inspire any employees to pursue his applications further.

The cruise

The good ship *The Emiliano* had sailed out of Los Angeles and was cruising around the Mexican Riviera according to schedule. Having taken a very active role in the shore excursion around the tequila factories of Puerto Vallarta, Susan Ratcliffe had returned to the boat's dining area and ordered some extra-spicy tacos. In fact she felt a bit worse for wear. It seemed that the enthusiasm she had undertaken for an education in local tequila varieties had proven to be ill-advised, taking into consideration the heat. However, the first few days of the holiday had been uneventful and she'd failed to ensnare any of the young talent into the holiday romance she was anticipating. Subsequently, despite her fuzzy vision and mild headache, she was eyeing up the male content of the room to see if there was a suitably unattached male to prey upon. Specifically, one who would fit the crisp white sailor uniform that was hanging on the wardrobe door in her cabin.

As Susan was trying to focus on the waiter bringing her tacos, and wishing he was an unattached sailor, Jonathan Fairchild was sitting at a bar at the other end of the dining area, sipping a double scotch. He was sitting alone on his bar-stool and in essence was facing a similar predicament, albeit non-sailor related. Despite being an American millionaire and major shareholder in *The Emiliano* he was attending his own cruise in considerable solitude.

It was unfortunate that, as Fairchild got up and turned to go to the bathroom, he knocked the arm of Susan as she was frantically ordering a Pina Colada to battle the burning sensation her spicy tacos had added to her other unpleasant tequila-induced sensations. A Pina Colada is a slightly sticky drink and therefore as it sloped over the white blouse of Susan it caused immense embarrassment for Jonathan Fairchild. However, for Susan this was an opportunity. It gave her both the opportunity to engage with the handsome fifty-something that she'd been at the bar next to, hoping for an 'in' to the conversation. It also provided an excuse to bully him into joining her for dinner once she'd changed. In addition to this, the spillage presented her with the opportunity to change into something a bit more seductive. The final and possibly main advantage to the whole event was that it also helped to disguise the fact that she already smelled quite heavily of tequila.

"At least I didn't knock you over," offered a red-faced and embarrassed Fairchild, who was torn between trying to help to mop up the spillage, and the idea that dabbing at the front of the woman's alcohol-stained blouse with a bar towel might add considerably to the embarrassment, rather than resolve the problem.

"Very true. Oh, I've come over all flush."

Susan started to do that ridiculous thing women do when they flap both hands in front of their face with the vigour of a startled pigeon, pretending to fan themselves. Fairchild tried to think of a sensible response.

"It's better to die on your feet than to live on your knees."

"I'm sorry!"

Fairchild had immediately regretted saying it as soon as it had come out of his mouth. What a stupid thing to say. However, it had been the maxim which had convinced him to go on the cruise in the first place and had been what he was thinking about just before he'd knocked into Susan.

"I said, 'it's better to die on your feet than to live on your knees'. Because I didn't knock you off your feet completely."

Susan looked confused and so Fairchild decided he would bumble on with the explanation, despite the Pina Colada having now run sufficiently down Susan so that it was dripping onto her feet.

"It's what Zapata, the Mexican revolutionary used to say."

"I love your moustache."

Jonathan tweezed the end of his elaborate whiskers between his left thumb and forefinger and used his right hand to click his fingers at the waiter, and ordered another drink for Susan.

"Let me get you a new drink while you get changed. After perhaps you'd like to join me for dinner, by way of apology."

Susan fluttered her eyelids before rushing off to her cabin to slip into something a bit more racy.

Fairchild's hero was Zapata. This was a man who had fought for the rights of the common man against the fat land owners of the Haciendas. The peasants lived in poverty and Zapata had dedicated his life to fight for their right to land and dignity. In his youth, Fairchild had fought for the rights of the local people of Ohio and made sure that people working in the factory he'd inherited got a fare wage and were treated with respect. He then went on to apply this principle to the other companies he had inherited from his hard-hearted father. He didn't greatly contribute to the profits of the companies he owned through this endeavour, although his wealth was so extreme he would never notice. However, he had achieved both a modicum of respect from the few workers who were aware of the effort he made. His only other achievement was a very striking moustache, which he considered to be a tribute to the great man himself.

The cook

Antonio De Luca, or Tony Lucas, was once an accomplished pizza chef, originally from Milton Keynes.

Tony Lucas had gravitated to the big smoke-city, and been trained to work as a chef in an Italian restaurant. In a very similar situation to Vince and his Michael Caine syndrome, Tony Lucas was actually encouraged to speak with an Italian accent to add an element of authenticity to his dough spinning antics on the Kensington high street. Until an unfortunate incident after work in the pantry, involving the boss's daughter-in-law, a jar of pickled herrings, two litres of olive oil and the necessity to call an ambulance, Tony had been on the way to a fruitful career. Despite losing his job he had chosen to retain his stage name and dodgy accent.

At the Armstrong Hotel, he insisted on pretending to be an extravagant Italian chef, despite getting up at 5.30am every morning for the last eleven years to fry out-of-date sausages for American tourists. His enthusiasm never waned, however, and was fuelled by the fact that his down time coincided with the long-running fad of filling day-time TV with cookery programmes. As a chef, albeit a greasy-spoon one, this emphasis on his trade in the media gave him an elevated sense of importance and he ran his kitchen as if there were a live TV audience to witness his cooking performance. In reality his captive on-lookers were a group of poorly paid Polish women who were, at best, confused by this extravagant posing and over-the-top arm waving. The elaborate gestures towards the industrial-sized toaster with his spatula, accompanied by sentences with the last two words having either an 'a' or an 'o' tackled on the end for 'Italiana effecto' were not appreciated to the extent he dreamed of. As a result, he was marginally more frustrated in his role than the people that had to work for him.

From a management perspective, Vince could find very little to complain about when it came to Antonio De Luca. He was always on time and created his meals with a passion. Even Vince could see that he wasn't Italian, which made it slightly frustrating if you were in a hurry. Waiting for an Englishman to finalise his convoluted sentence because he was trying to make it more European, did feel like a waste of time when there were other things to do. De Luca did do a good fried breakfast though, which was all that was asked of him.

Reflection

Susan sat at breakfast gazing dreamily at her new man. Alan, her former husband and pretend officer of the cavalry, would never have had the education or refinement to quote Mexican revolutionaries. He only knew about Custer because he liked cowboy and Indian films and wearing a pretend gun. No, her new man was something special and this was a life-changing moment. She would be his, and try to live by his high moral codes. She mentally complimented herself as she took this moral stance and applied some butter to her second warm croissant of the morning.

Fairchild smiled back with the air of a man who was content. It was at that moment that Susan thought of the several underpaid and slightly absent-of-legal-entitlement Polish girls who scrubbed the floors of the Armstrong Hotel each day. She was immediately horrified, and accidentally allowed butter to drip onto her red bikini top. Susan Ratcliffe was the capitalist landlord of the Armstrong hacienda. Fairchild would be shocked to find out he had been seeing a woman of such low morality. He had spent his life taking down people just like her. She could not allow herself to waste this opportunity or the cruise ticket. How would she hold on to her new dreamy hunk and deal with the situation back in Paddington? It was very difficult to hide the fact that all her staff were employed illegally, and to do so in such a short space of time. Especially as she was not there to do it herself.

Fairchild left to use the bathroom in his cabin, so Susan decided to go to the phones and call up Warwick Masterton. Several attempts later it was clear he wasn't answering his mobile. At the reception she only got the idiot kid, Vincent. There was no point trying to plot with him to disguise her hotel to look like one that employed people legally. He and his Polish girlfriend were part of the problem, not the solution. There were three days left of the cruise, and so she had three days to come up with a plan.

The guests

Marvin Fletcher and Laurence Thompson were businessmen. More importantly, they were crooked businessmen, which is why they were acquainted with Warwick Masterton. Back in the East Midlands they had been largely involved in 'property crime'. This included anything from dealing in electronics that had fallen off the back of lorries, adding to the auto-part sector by helping to steal cars and break them up for parts, and using the cross-channel ferry to help them dabble in tax free alcohol from the continent.

More recently, the man they were now expected to refer to as 'Warwick Masterton' had set them up with some business links in London. Warwick would make the contacts. He had come across similar 'businessmen' who were slightly bigger fish and wanted to expand northwards. Linking up his new London contacts with the likes of Marvin and Laurence was equally beneficial to all. For Warwick, it meant that he got cash for making the introductions. This was good money but without ever seeing a stolen good or directly committing a crime. It was a process that fitted well with his current need for anonymity outside the circles of his current identity.

Marvin and Laurence arrived at the Armstrong Hotel at around four in the afternoon that Friday, having travelled down from Coventry. As usual they arrived at reception and asked the idiot kid, who was always trying to sound like Bob Hoskins, to fetch Masterton for them. To their surprise, the kid told them that Masterton was away. Marvin made some excuse about not having his driving license with him and pointed out that, as he was a regular guest, it shouldn't matter. Vince was aware that these guys were always signed in by Masterton and so decided it was better not to make a fuss. He offered to have a look in the files later and find the old copies of their IDs to help him fill in the registry. The two men agreed to this and headed up to their usual rooms on the second floor, looking very disgruntled.

Once they were behind closed doors, Marvin immediately tried to reach Masterton on his mobile. Not only was he furious about the inconvenience that this had caused, but also they didn't know who they were supposed to be. They were so used to Masterton sorting out their paperwork for them at the hotel that it had never been necessary for them to be aware of what their false identity actually was.

After several attempts it was clear that Masterton wasn't picking up his mobile phone. Frustrated, they both departed the hotel in different directions. Each one had a night of business to attend to before they met again in the morning for a joint business venture with a very dodgy guy in Paddington.

The suppliers

Vince started his shift behind the desk the next morning at 7.00am, only to find Kaleena already waiting for him.

"Yam right there Kaleena? Shouldn't yaw be down in the kitchens like?"

"It is the chef, Antonio. He big problem. Some insect with leg in kitchen. Maybe you come see?"

Kaleena led the way to the lower floor, through the dining area and into the kitchen.

"Gooda morningo, Vince-a!"

"Hello Mr De Luca, Kaleena said you needed some help. Is it to do with supplies or something like that. I'll see what I can do, but I'd thought we were okay for a week or so."

"Antonio, Antonio, please-a. No more of this Mr Luca! Supplies you say, arr Vince! If only this were-a true-o. No, but we have bigga problemo."

"What's happened, Antonio?"

Fortunately Vince was born with a modicum of patience. Antonio's delusion that he was constantly performing to a live audience and camera situated by the door to the dining area meant that it took him a long time to say anything.

"What's-a happened-a? What's-a happened you-a say! I tell you what's-a happened! It is the cock-a-rach. Never before in the kitchen of Antonio De Luca. Now we have-a the cock-a-rach in the store, in the cupboardo…everywhere…o!"

By this time Antonio was wildly waving his spatula about and combined this with a series of half-pirouette type manoeuvres to help demonstrate where 'everywhere-o' might include.

"It is a disastero. Never in my life did I see!"

"Where do you think these cockroaches are all suddenly coming from then, Antonio?"

It is the sausages. I say to Mrs A-Ratt-a-cliffe. Why you no buya the gooda sausage? Why you no buy from the nice-a people? But she say 'no, Antonio. We musta make-a the save, and buy-a the cheap'. Vince, now you musta go and find the poison for the cock-a-rach. You musta buy the new sausage for-a replace. Where is the money to be saved in this? I ask you?"

Vince got the message, which was emphasised by an over-elaborate shrug from Antonio at the end of his performance: cockroach spray and a new box of sausages. Was it really necessary to go through that whole performance to be asked to buy a couple of things?

"Not to worry, Antonio. I'll pop to the shops now for you."

Having established the quantity of sausages to be replaced, Vince grabbed his coat and headed out into the cool spring morning to find a butcher and some industrial strength insect spray.

The cleaning routine

Check-out for the hotel guests was at 10.00am. It was only after this time that Kaleena and the others got the privilege of cleaning the rooms. A romantic weekend in the capital on the cheap was often accompanied by a combination of rekindled love, over-indulgence of drinks people wouldn't normally drink, and food that disagreed with them. Appreciating the extent of each of these components was a skill that Kaleena and her colleagues had quickly acquired, and not one they relished. As a result, the task of cleaning the rooms was not the most sought after of all the jobs for the hired help. The early nature of this routine was to enable Kaleena and the other three Polish girls that did the cleaning to get around all of the rooms before the check-in of new guests at 3.00pm. A more amply staffed establishment might have been able to cope with a later checkout time but 10.00am was fairly standard for the cheaper places.

It was with her usual sense of apathy that Kaleena used the skeleton key to open the door of room 2-0-2, and reversed her way in. She dragged her mop and box of cleaning equipment behind her using her back to keep open the spring loaded door. As she turned, Kaleena found herself faced with the unusual sight of three men, one of them in the chair, one of them sitting on the end of the bed and another standing by the window. There was one open briefcase with money in it next to the man on the bed, and there was a closed briefcase on the lap of the second gentlemen in the chair. Overall, the men did not look pleased that they had been interrupted. Kaleena was no fool. Russian mafia films with Polish dubbing regularly held scenes like this in it. Normally at least one man would have a scar on his face and wear a leather jacket. Despite the absence of this key character, Kaleena decided that this was not a good place to be. Unfortunately, in her surprise, she had let go of the spring loaded door, and just as she was about to make a quick exit it crashed into her mop and bucket, sending a flood of soapy water back into the corridor. It was to her benefit that she then made lots of garbled excuses in Polish whilst mopping the small puddle by the door before closing it and starting on the mess in the corridor.

At least the two men would have the comfort of believing she didn't have the language skills to tell anyone what she'd seen.

It was something of an unwritten law that the 10.00am checkout didn't apply to Warwick's friends. Sometimes their business required them to remain until early afternoon. Vince knew this. What he didn't know was that Warwick always made a point of telling the cleaners his friends were staying, which rooms his friends were in, and for them to keep well away. Once they had checked-out at the desk, left the hotel and returned their keys, Warwick would then give permission for the cleaners to enter the rooms.

Marvin and Laurence

Marvin and Laurence had seen a lot of dodgy mafia films in their time as well. It was something of an interest to them. The Hollywood greats of Al Pacino and the like, hoodwinking big city crooks and making them 'sleep with the fishes' to send a threatening message was a keen interest. However, when your illegal network is straddled between Paddington and Coventry, and your biggest risk is missing the connection at Galton Bridge, then it's rare you actually apply the gangland stories to your daily life. Despite this, a cleaner bursting in on a deal, yabbering in some foreign language, and then kicking her bucket over to extend the time she stayed in the room to study the goings on, was a bit of a wake-up call.

The man in the chair slowly got up, his briefcase still closed. He took his black overcoat from the back of the chair and placed it over his arm. He looked at Marvin with a thunderous expression, which suggested he would not be working with amateurs, and then left the room without saying a word.

His dramatic departure was followed by a lengthy and animated argument between Marvin and Laurence over the failure to close the deal. People back in Coventry would not be pleased, and there was going to be some serious explaining to do.

The second animated argument revolved around what to do about the cleaner. Sure she had seen the money, but not seen inside the second briefcase. More the pity, Marvin and Laurence hadn't either. Had she seen the face of their business associate for long enough to recognise him again? If she was working for some rival Russian gang then they were in trouble. If she was really a cleaner whom the police might call on as a witness in a line-up then she had to be silenced. They were going to be in enough trouble with the guys in Coventry for not closing the deal. This would be the least of their worries if the mob at the Paddington end thought they'd put their operation at risk.

Eventually they reached an agreement. The key to all of this was the kid on reception. He would need to find the girl for them. Depending on the outcome they would then have to find someone in their line of work who spoke Russian to come and 'persuade' her to keep quiet about what she'd seen. They could take no risks and so they would need to find a new place to stay as well, until this all blew over.

Escape

Kaleena was frantically rushing about in the room on the top floor of the hotel that she and Vince shared. She was rapidly stuffing the little she owned into her neon-pink suitcase, which was already part-filled with the various orders of London goods placed by her mother in Poland. All she knew was that it was not safe to be in the Armstrong Hotel for a minute longer. She struggled to lift up the small window, made difficult by years of the wooden frame warping in a coating of peeling white gloss. As she climbed out onto the wobbly wrought-iron fire escape, she looked down to examine her immediate journey. The steps were intact but clearly she was the first person to use these stairs in years. Kaleena started gingerly down the first set, noting the differing degrees to which the wall attachments fulfilled their roles, and the extent to which the whole assemblage wobbled every time she moved.

In her panic, her hearing didn't register the loud clunking as she dragged her pink suitcase behind her down the thin steps. The unexpected noise meant that an illicit affair in room 402 was temporarily interrupted. This was much to the frustration of a man called Clive, who was down to his underpants and regretting that he was still maintaining a shroud of secrecy between himself and his lover over the fact that he was wearing a toupee. The interruption of a pink suitcase clattering past their fourth floor window to the tune of thud against metal did little to boost his confidence.

The fact that Kaleena was also about to pass by the room occupied by Warwick Masterton's guests on the second floor, also failed to register in her planning.

The explosion

The explosion reverberated around the hotel from the basement to the roof. The range of impacts that it had on various people in the vicinity was remarkable. For Kaleena, the iron staircase rattled and she doubled her speed for fear of it crumbling beneath her. As luck would have it, the explosion sent shivers down the frayed nerves of the dodgy occupants of room 202. The two of them had also been packing their bags in light of recent events. Their next stop was to confront Vince to ensure steps were taken to silence the cleaning girl. The explosion had been a catalyst for an early departure and they were closing the door behind them just as Kaleena rattled at high speed in a pink blur passed their open window. For Clive in room 402, the explosion assisted greatly in raising his new lover's opinion of him, as well as his own self esteem. It also turned out to be a definitive moment in solving his dilemma of when to admit to the toupee.

Vince had been sitting behind the desk at reception. Following what sounded like a small bomb going off from somewhere beneath him, he immediately rushed down to the kitchen in the basement. He had never experienced such a trail of carnage. Firstly there was a train of soft rolls, marmalade portions and salt cellars making an exodus from the open kitchen door across to the far reaches of the dining room. The kitchen was a collage of broken crockery and splats of diced fruit. Almost everything that had ever been hanging up on a shelf or on a surface had fallen, and most was now on the floor in varying states of disrepair.

Antonio De Luca lay on the floor in the corner by the fridge-freezer. At first glance, Vince thought he'd had his guts torn apart by what had happened, but closer inspection showed that a large open tin of diced plum tomatoes had fallen on him, followed by a string of mini-sausages. Antonio called him over with the air of one who was in a bad play and about to use his last breath to reveal the murderer before croaking. Vince obliged by crunching his way across the floor to where he lay.

"What on earth has happened, Mr De Luca?"

"It was the Cock-a-rach. I spray-a the cock-a-rach on the oven and then a boom. It has a crisis. The flame of the gas exploda the can."

Antonio pointed at the gas stove and then did an elaborate boom-type gesture with his hands, accidently spraying Vince with plum tomato juice. Antonio then made a further gesture to the area next to the stove where a pile of paper napkins was happily burning. The can of insect spray itself was nowhere to be seen.

"Vincent. Quickly now, you musta put out-a the fire!"

Despite all that was going on, Vince somehow found time to be amazed that, despite the accident, Antonia was still keeping up the charade of his Italian accent.

"No problem, Mr De Luca. I'll do that now for ya."

The fire was small and as it was on a stainless steel surface the threat was not immediate. However, to help to calm down the pseudo-Italian in his tomatoey covering, Vince took the fire-extinguisher from the floor, pulled the pin and pointed the nozzle in the direction of the flames.

Caveman technology

The cavemen who discovered fire were the nuclear physicists of their day. Revered by all who were more simple-minded, they were the envy of all those who stood in awe of their technological breakthrough but didn't really understand it.

As a science, our understanding of the concept of fire amongst generations of the human race has been almost unshakeable for millennia. Stuff like wood, burned with fire. Pouring water on it, and making it wet, stopped the fire. Simple. However, one of the most remarkable things about science is that it is continually evolving. New truths emerge and old ones are forgotten. As our understanding changes, it seems that so does the science itself. What you had taken as gospel previously was now little more than a laughable joke about our thick ancestors. For example, the paradigm of global climate in the mid-20th century was that we were on the brink of plunging into an ice-age so that the oceans would retract and the ice shelves would grow. By the end of the century, the human race was more concerned that things were going to warm up so rapidly that we'd have to escape the rising seas by using what remained of the forest to build arks. Similarly, there was a time with $E=mc^2$, when it always did. Now, with string theory and dark matter, it seems we must be open to possible exceptions to this certainty.

The science of fire and water had been one of the few unshakeable truths of generations of academia. However, more recently, along with lots of other stuff, it has turned out that this long accepted relationship is largely nonsense. This was also the conclusion that Vince rapidly reached as the wide jet of water from his cheap fire extinguisher splashed over the top of the burning napkins and into the two deep-fat fryers.

The fireball

Marvin and Laurence arrived at the reception desk, each with suitcase in hand. They were ready for action and would take the receptionist out back and rough him up a bit if they had to. This was not a time for half-measures. It was just as Marvin banged a firm and menacing hand on the small bell beside the registry book that a large fireball, accompanied by a thunderous whoosh and warm orange glow, passed dramatically behind them. It was making rapid progress from the basement and headed up the next flight of stairs in the direction of the first floor. Slightly gobsmacked by this, the two of them stood open-jawed, staring at the staircase that they had just descended waiting to see if it would happen again, or indeed what would happen next. As soon as time became reanimated, it quickly became apparent that the next exciting instalment of events was the commencement of the aging fire-alarm, an extension of which was situated above their heads. Being old and rarely called upon, the alarm seemed to take a few goes at waking up and really getting into its role. A bit like an old petrol lawnmower that was perfectly happy in a dusty corner of the shed believing it had been retired, and then being dragged out for its first post-winter outing. By the time the alarm had gained enough momentum to genuinely reinforce the idea that something was wrong, Marvin and Laurence were already heading, with determination, for the front door. Alarms meant police, and police meant they needed to be long gone and never look back.

Vince had been very surprised by the result of his actions. His expectation was that a garden hose-like spray of water would put out the small pile of fiery-napkins, and he would then help Antonio from under his pile of tomatoes before searching the remaining crockery for any other underpaid survivors of the explosion. What actually happened was a towering column of flame that looked like it was being fired from the bowels of a volcano. The flame then spread across the entire ceiling before finding the gap over the dining room door and whooshing out into the wider world. Vince was left with quite a lot of smoke, a considerable fire in the chip pans, as well as several flaming cupboards.

Antonio was apparently not as detrimentally affected by the previous explosion as he had first imagined, and was already on his feet and heading at high speed for the side door. Vince decided it might be wise if he followed him.

Susan's return

Susan Ratcliffe and Jonathan Fairchild had arrived at Heathrow Airport and made their way back to the hotel by black-cab, as Fairchild had never been to England before and had always wanted to have a go in one. It had been an impulsive decision on Fairchild's part to travel to the United Kingdom, home of his new found love. He was not often a spontaneous man but the way his emotions were flowing at the moment he felt like there was nothing he couldn't do. From Susan's perspective, this had been the result of days in carefully crafted manipulation of an indecisive and unspontaneous man with a strong jaw line and a large bank account.

Fairchild was engrossed in the new experience of the black-cab, and Susan was engrossed with the vision of his strong jaw line. It was therefore only when the cabbie pointed out to them that he couldn't get any closer to the hotel because of all of the emergency services blocking the road, that Susan began to suspect that something was wrong.

Susan and Fairchild joined the hotel guests and other residents of the street on the opposite side of the road to the Armstrong Hotel, and watched the spectacle. Firemen in breathing apparatus filed out of the front of the smoky hotel entrance, evidently having extinguished anything that had been set alight as a result of the fireball. Gradually the firemen departed in their red truck, and the crowds dispersed.

Susan was not as devastated by this vision as she might have been. Her contemplation of the situation meant that she was harbouring two key thoughts. Firstly, she'd never noticed before how fetching a fireman looked in his uniform, despite its initial un-shapeliness. Secondly, the gutting of her hotel by a random fireball could very well play out perfectly to solve all of her current problems. She had been out of the country and had left Masterton in charge. Therefore, she would not be under any suspicion of foul-play which meant the insurance company would have to pay up. This would mean that she could get out of the hotel business with a shed-load of money in the bank, take an early retirement, and travel the world with Fairchild. It also meant that she no longer employed the sort of people who would have inspired Zapata to single her out for a targeted revolution.

Having calculated her future prospects, and decided they'd never looked better, Susan gazed tearfully at Fairchild and began to sob into his chest. Fairchild had never felt so needed and protective of anyone before in his life.

Heathrow

Kaleena arrived at Heathrow Airport with her rapidly packed suitcase. She now appreciated the convenience of the underground rail-link between Paddington and the airport. Having made her way from the depths of the underground to the check-in area, she approached one of the desks that managed ticket sales. A flight to Poland, via anywhere but here, was all that was on her mind.

To her surprise she was greeted by a man who looked remarkably like the manager of the hotel she had just left. Was it not for him sounding so different, she would have sworn it was the same man. Having done a double-take she checked his name tag: 'Jules Leamington'.

"Where would ya care to flight to today, ma'am?" The body-double of Masterton offered in his gentile Irish brogue.

"Warsaw. I go Warsaw. Next fly."

"Ah, Poland. A beautiful place though I say so myself. I have a special offer on the luggage transit to there, ma'am, if a can tempt you into saving some of your hard earned money. We sell you a ticket with no check-in luggage for about half the price, and then ship your bags out to you a few days later for next to nothing. Can't be bad now can it."

Kaleena was already in a very suspicious frame and paranoid state of mind, and had had enough of dodgy carryings-on for one day. Parting with your luggage unnecessarily seemed, at best, like a scam to nick your luggage, and at worse, then some kind of smuggling operation using your suitcase to move illegal goods across borders. She chose not to take advantage of the special offer and decided her bags would accompany her all the way.

Chapter 4 –Mini-cab

The next trade

It was fortunate that the fire-ball that Vince had created from the kitchens of the Armstrong Hotel had not quite reached the fourth floor. Therefore, the room at the top of the building that Vince and Kaleena had stayed in was largely un-scorched by the extreme bolt of angry flame, or the more conventional fire that then followed. This of course did not include the minor pre-existing fire damage in his room, which was the reason that the upper rooms had not previously been available to hotel guests and instead were available for staff to rent. Vince suspected that this policy would change now that the majority of the hotel required a full refurbishment. His belongings, all be them few, remained intact. As he packed up his things, Vince reflected on the 'Dear John' letter he had been left by Kaleena:

Dear Vince,

I go away. You never see me again. I find bad man in hotel. Mafia. Like Russian movie. It not safe I stay.

Love you always.

Your Kaleena.

He folded the brief soliloquy and put it in the side pocket of his bag. He was sad in one way that she was gone. He knew that she cared for him in her slightly quirky way. However, she had been a big distraction from the trade-up plan. Kaleena was the first semi-committed relationship Vince had been in, and subsequently she had stretched across two trade-ups, which was a considerable deviation to the trade-up rules, particularly so early on. He was going to have to toughen up and learn from this.

Vince was now back on his own, there were no distractions, he had a grasp for life in the capital city, and he already had his next trade-up worked out. With renewed commitment to stepping into a better life, Vince sloshed his way out of the damp and charred lobby of the Armstrong Hotel and headed for a bedsit in Whitechapel at the top floor of a building owned by a Polish guy called Gustav, who he had met though Kaleena's London friends.

There are urban legends in London about black-cab drivers 'doin the knowledge' so that they know exactly where every street is, and the best way to get there. This, Vince had concluded, helped justify their extortionate rates. However, the myth was disproved by Vince in his first and only cab ride. He and Kaleena had gone to visit Gustav: a friend of a friend of Kaleena's who was helping to organise her some fake Polish qualifications so she could apply for a job that didn't involve unclogging chunks of vomit out of hotel shower drains. Having stated the address they were aiming for, the cabby declared it didn't exist, and had handed them an A-to-Z map asking them to find the place and give direction. For the return journey, disillusioned with black-cabs, and considerably less well off (there had been no discount for navigation), they had taken a mini-cab back. Surprisingly, this was even less successful than the black-cab. The driver arrived forty minutes late in a very musky smelling Toyota Corolla. He spoke no languages common to either Vince or Kaleena, and seemed to spend almost an hour circling the Paddington area, evidently looking for a way in. At the time, neither was impressed with the service. However, Vince had since decided it might be a good filler-job whilst looking for better things. On reflection, in the absence of a UK driving licence, any driving experience and a limited understanding of the layout of the city, Vince was at least equally qualified for the position, and his language skills might even be the edge that would get him a job.

There were three simple tasks to perform before he could apply for a mini-cab driver job. One, get a driving licence; two, learn to drive, and three, learn his way around London. The driving licence was simple enough. He'd moved into a room in Whitechapel above the flat of Gustav, the Polish guy who forged academic qualifications. Vince made arrangements with Gustav. For a price, the forger would source a Polish driving licence for him. The license didn't even have to be a particularly good forgery. It would appear to be a document from an EU country and so perfectly valid in the UK, but completely incomprehensible to most employers who would not be able to argue about its authenticity. From their perspective, later on should there be a run in with the authorities about the employee, they could blame Vince for falsifying documents, so the risk was minimal. Gustav also added in a few other documents (private hire license and topographical assessment) as part of the deal. Challenge one was therefore solved.

For task number two, Vince took three very cheap driving lessons from Gustav. Gustav was a heavy-set man who drove an equally heavy set Eastern European pre-unification vehicle, called an FSO Polonez, with the steering wheel positioned on the wrong side of the car. Vince had decided that lessons from Gustav would be an advantage, both due to the low cost of the lessons and the opportunity for a Polish-based driving experience anecdote to embellish his driving licence story. Of course it was possible Vince was going to have to feign a tinge of a Polish accent when he talked. Fortunately his broad Midland's accent was regularly received in London as if he'd come from some far off, unintelligible land, so it was unlikely to be a problem. Three lessons seemed adequate to master the physical controls of the FSO. Vince already knew about gears and things from playing on Ed Symond's game-station after school, when they had been doing their GCSEs. London was mainly a traffic jam of slow suburban roads with 30 mile an hour speed limits, so it was not like he needed to develop any significant skills at driving beyond the basics.

The third and final challenge was 'the knowledge'. Not coming from London, Vince's awareness of the vast metropolis currently extended to the area around Paddington station and a couple of streets in Whitechapel. However, one thing Vince had been subject to throughout his life was a need to use suburban bus routes to move around, during his Midlands up-bringing. Subsequently, he knew how the town council bus route planning worked, which by and large totally contradicted the need. Public transport was often at the forefront of local politics, with people that would never actually get on a bus in a month of Sundays, but who would be regularly up in arms if a bus was re-routed from their neighbourhood. Just because they didn't use it was irrelevant, they paid their council tax and so it was there constitutional right for a half empty bus to go past their house three times a week. Subsequently, buses serving the outlying areas always took the most tedious and unnecessary route to get to where they were going, so that they unnecessarily drove past the unused bus-stops of every middle-class tax-paying lobbyist. Vince, map in hand, spent five days taking buses to several unlikely corners of the city and, in the process, received a very convincing overview of most of the road network of London.

Just two weeks after the fire at the hotel, Vince was actively seeking work in London as a professional driver.

Derek's Mini-cabs

Vince was offered the first driving job that he had applied for. His boss, Derek, (of Derek's Mini-cab Hire) had concluded that he was just the sort of go-getter they needed at the firm, and he could start immediately. Vince had failed to be suspicious of this enthusiasm. In hindsight his ability to exude 'go' and 'gettingness' had not always been a strength that he would declare in an interview that he could bring to a job. He only had Derek's word for it that he'd given such an impression on this occasion. Subsequently, Vince's first day at work was a bit of a disappointment.

His initial let down was the realisation that he had tried too hard in his pre-cabby preparation, and wasted a lot of time and money on forged documentation. The dodgy mini-cab firm had welcomed him with open arms and not even paid enough attention to his fake paperwork to notice that they wouldn't be able to understand it. Secondly, he discovered he was going to be charged sixty quid a week to be given driving jobs by the mini-cab firm. In addition, it was clear that the hours would be unsociable, and that he would have to provide his own car. This last revelation was quite a surprise. So far in life Vince had found that employers were the ones to equip employees to carry out low paid and degrading tasks, not the other way around. He pointed this out to one of the other mini-cab drivers. It was explained that if he wanted to go and be a freelance taxi driver the only way in London was to drive a black-cab, and that was a whole different closed shop as far as the likes of them were concerned.

Consequently, Vince became one of a very select club of mini-cab drivers whose limousine of choice was a right-hand drive FSO Polonez. Also, he had to pay Gustav the Pole thirty quid a week to borrow it, and agree to make sure it was filled with petrol each time he returned it. Not only was he down ninety quid a week before he started, he also had to agree that he would drive Gustav and his shady associates around in-between jobs if required. One of Gustav's many questionable functions was sourcing fake documents, and there were always at least two or three dodgy business associates in the apartment at any one time, drinking schnapps and talking in low growls from behind their dark and sunken eyes. Subsequently, there was a limit to which Vince really wanted to start being the professional driver for him and his shadowy alcoholics. However, right now his choices seemed limited.

Charity starts with Fairchild

Jonathan Fairchild, with a little coaxing from his new found love, Susan Ratcliffe, had taken to British society like a duck to water. He had immediately rented an expensive flat in Knightsbridge and was looking to buy something more permanent overlooking the Thames. Through invitations to various social events and charity fund raising evenings, he had rapidly developed a close circle of friends that were looking for ways to tap into his enormous overseas wealth. These new extravagant social appointments meant that Susan had subsequently developed a wardrobe full of evening gowns and expensive jewellery. If sold off, Susan's new wardrobe could support a small charity on its own, without the need to attend the high society fund raising events.

One such entrepreneur, who was looking to befriend Jonathan Fairchild and tap in to his enormous wealth, was Ted Renwick. Ted had happened across Fairchild at a celebrity event, where costumes from by-gone London operas were being auctioned off to wealthy and famous investors in support of a children's charity. It was remarkable that they had both so much in common, and was as if they were destined to meet and become firm friends. Ted somehow knew all about Ohio and all about the Mexican Riviera as well. He sympathised with Fairchild's need to be a responsible boss, and to look after the little people in this world. Renwick felt very much the same, and when running his own businesses he was also trying to give back to society as much as he got out of it. Meanwhile, Ted's wife, Sheila, was a London girl like Susan. They shared the same interest in shopping and dress designers. They both had a love for tequila and raucous laughter for the benefit of all in the room rather than the appreciation of a joke. They also had a similar disregard for hard work. Susan and Sheila rapidly became inseparable, and the four of them double-dated several times a week. Fairchild had never questioned why it happened that Ted and he were such compatible buddies. England was adorable, Susan was wonderful, English and adorable, and so were the little people of London. It never occurred to him that the pre-hustle Ted had really done his homework on Fairchild. Susan was equally remiss in spotting the fraudster, as she was far too busy making sure her talons were deep enough into Fairchild to avoid separation from her new and wealthy man.

On-call

Vince's first night as a mini-cab driver had gone okay. His first job of the evening was to pick up a couple from Islington and take them to the London City Airport. There was a look of shock on the faces of these well-to-do, middle-aged professionals as they wheeled their cabin bags through the front door. They watched with concern as Vince carefully unwound the wire that held the hatchback in place so it could slowly rise to a height where the gap was big enough to get the luggage in. The wife quietly scolded her husband who should have got a black-cab like she told him in the first place. Before she had chance to refuse the service, Vince politely opened the rear left door for her and muttered the Polish for 'please bring back another cold one from the fridge'. This was one of the key phrases he'd been taught by Kaleena, and more latterly been subject to during his association with Gustav. It worked wonders.

Whilst angry with her husband, the woman was determined not to seem impolite to the foreign gentlemen who had been so gallant, as it further supported her silently erupting campaign against the husband who had ruined the weekend before it had even begun. This anger quickly commuted to concern for their safety as the driver got into the same side of the car as she had, and carefully drove off in third, determinedly following the edge of the drain with his front left tyre to avoid hitting anything coming the other way.

Vince tended to do most of his driving in the gutter as it was really difficult for him to judge from the wrong side of the car how much of the FSO was sticking out into the middle of the road and presenting a hazard to on-coming vehicles. Also, Vince tended to do most of his driving in third gear. First gear made strange noises and second had presumably fallen off somewhere in Poland before the car ever ventured into British territory. As the traffic never moved fast enough to get into fourth, third was clearly the gear of choice.

Having successfully deposited the couple at the airport, Vince's second task of the evening was to take some posh people to a play in the West-end. They were all dressed up in expensive evening finery, and similarly surprised to find themselves being chauffeured to their social event in the lime green FSO. The remainder of the night's work was driving pissed-up people to and from pubs, and then very pissed-up people to and from nightclubs.

By three in the morning, Vince was done. Parking in the street outside Gustav's, he used the water tap outside the ground floor flat to fill a bucket and throw it over the Vinyl back seat and plastic flooring of the car to remove any traces of vomit and spilt beer. It was an easy car to clean and the rust holes in the corner of the floor meant that the access water drained out quickly. Finally he left the back windows half open to help get the smell out, and then headed up to his bedsit. He'd made a £105, taking into account the ten he spent on petrol. So £5 profit so far, and the rest of the week's takings were just for him. However, he was starting to regret the deal he'd made with Gustav about car maintenance.

The remaining windscreen wiper was lacking the wiper part, and the left and right indicators were wired incorrectly. At first Vince just thought this was because the steering wheel was on the wrong side. However, as the night had progressed, he realised this wasn't the case, and it took a lot of concentrating to remember to indicate left when turning right. To describe the brakes as a bit 'spongy', would have been an insult to sponges. For the meantime, using them in combination with the handbrake seemed to do the trick. He suspected that wet-weather mini-cabbing was going to be a bit more challenging. Then again, making a profit in this new line of work would mean that he needed to avoid doing any work on the car what so ever.

Moving house for celebrities

Ted Renwick was a hustler and a schemer. He'd successfully pulled off a number of sneaky plays with the help of his team, which included his fake wife, Sheila. The trick with scheming was to be able to disappear immediately afterwards, leaving no trace that you had been there. Ted's current scheme had been knocking around inside his head for a few years but he'd never been able to set it up, as it involved a lot of transport, which was difficult to make disappear at the end. So, he couldn't believe his luck when a rich, naive American arrived on the scene with a middle-aged, slightly frumpy bimbo in tow. Fairchild's dull conversations almost always veered towards his boredom with his dull American business dealings and a desire to get into something more interesting and worthwhile. It was almost like he was looking for people to rip him off. Well, Ted Renwick and his team were happy to oblige.

The plan was as follows: Ted would start up a house moving company that was exclusively for the celebrities, rock-stars and A-listers. This was essentially a furniture removal company which would specialise in carefully shifting the antique possessions of the rich and famous from abode to posh abode. The service would have specialised vehicles to protect delicate priceless items and a trained team of staff who would know how best to wrap, parcel and protect all such goods whilst in transit. This service would not come cheap, but 10% of the profit would go to charity which would help the disgustingly rich feel good about upgrading from a ten to twenty million pound home. They would be increasing the wall space available for their expanding collection of antique masters, meanwhile, some orphan kids in a ghetto somewhere would receive a one dollar injection against Tetanus, and a leaflet with a cartoon of a kid being injected on it that they could nail to the mud wall of their shanty squalor; so it was win-win all round.

Renwick's scheme was ingenious. The service would operate for a few months with the outward appearance of a genuine business – but without actually doing very much. Through networking and social gatherings, he would build a reputation as the only real choice for house moving by the nouveau riche that demanded the highest quality service for their bling. Gradually, as more and more important clients became interested, Renwick planned that all removal vans would need to be in operation at the same time and on the same day – filled with antiques. At which point, the team of thieves would make for various locked garages and places to stash the fortune, then dump the vehicles and assume a low profile from which to gradually cash in on the fortune.

Renwick had the fake business up and running; there was a pretend office with a secretary, a fake website with fake emails and so on. All of which was easy to make disappear without a trace at the scent of someone tumbling the hustle. He didn't even need a fake bank account, as payment would be made after the service was complete. This would never be the case as Renwick would have stashed all the antiques long before anyone was required to get the cheque book out. He had schmoozed his way around enough celebrity charity events to develop his client base. He also had long standing and well developed networks for shifting antiques of dubious origin. The problem was that, unlike the fake business, it was the hardware (i.e. the vans), that were more difficult to dispose of with no traces. What he lacked was a fleet of vehicles which were impressive enough to be the transport for the belongings of celebs, but the papers of which could in no way be linked to him or his crew, should they be discovered containing any stolen antiques. He could not hire the trucks. If he paid cash up front the company would be suspicious and either report him or want to get in on the action. He could not hire the trucks using a bank account without it being traceable. He could not buy trucks for similar reasons. Stealing several new trucks was out of the question. They would stand out like a sore thumb.

This is where the generous and immensely patriotic Jonathan Fairchild would come in. Renwick would convince him that if Fairchild could help them buy the new fleet of special vans and trucks, the investment would quickly more than equal the amount they could help contribute to charity. Being a proud American was essential, as he would be told that the best trucks were in America and as a respected citizen, Fairchild could help him to import them. This was ideal, as there was no way Fairchild could just give the money over, he would be convinced that he would have to return to the states for the actual purchase. Renwick would then make out to Fairchild that the new trucks were registered to the company. He would put fake number plates on them, and get the job done almost immediately before anyone became suspicious. Once the abandoned trucks were discovered some time later – the only person they could be linked to would be Fairchild.

Fairchild was the perfect target. He was incredibly rich, American, and newly arrived in London. He was also a regular at charity events. His business sense was not particularly sharp, and his money was largely inherited, rather than resulting from any sharp business dealings of his own. Finally, he seemed strangely smitten with an overly made-up, permed woman, who poured herself into evening gowns that were designed for people with different figures to that of her own particular shape. On this basis, Fairchild was more likely to make a generous charitable gesture to impress the curly-headed gold digger swinging from his arm, than to pay too much attention to where his charitable donation was going.

Gustav the Pole

Vince had been a mini-cab driver for a few weeks, and was rapidly becoming the official driver for Gustav and his heavies. Probably 25% of his work was actually doing jobs for Gustav's company, whatever that was. Vince assumed it was either something to do with drugs or tax evasion, but had decided it was much easier, and ultimately more healthy for him, not to ask too many questions. He came from a back-water in the Midlands where he had never been exposed to any real crime or underworld type stuff. However, he knew enough to realise that the less you know or say about something, the less of a risk you became to anyone. Consequently, he was developing a real talent for looking the other way, and especially for keeping shtum. Recent examples of keeping shtum included maintaining his silence regarding his part in burning down a Paddington guesthouse, stitching up his co-workers at the factory with his out-sourcing plan, and his misadventure with Natalie Sedgwick. The details of the latter still remained somewhat uncertain, but continued to be a subject that was not to be raised.

Vince was actually enjoying his mini-cab work. He had really taken to driving, and after a few weeks had perfected the art of operating a right-hand-drive car without terrifying all of his customers. In addition, mini-cabbing got him 'out and about', meeting new people, and presented different tasks each time. It was almost the opposite to working in a brake-cable factory, and Vince really did appreciate the difference. He had even renegotiated the thirty quid deal with Gustav the Pole for mini-cabbing in his Polonez. He was now actually getting paid extra for driving Gustav's dodgy mates, who seemed to be delivering packages and documents all over London. Gustav even sometimes booked Vince via the mini-cab firm on the basis he could fiddle the books.

Gustav was also really appreciating Vince as his business driver. For a start, the Polonez was a clapped-out old bomb from Poland, and not a pleasurable driving experience. Gustav was determined that the next time that he drove a car it would be a Mercedes Benz. However, the very fact that the car was a clapped-out old bomb from Poland was why he had it. In Gustav's line of work, keeping a low profile was important. A foreigner cruising around in a shiny Merc in Whitechapel was going to draw attention. However, the FSO was not. The challenge was that none of his associates, who had vacated a country with a questionable national car, were actually prepared to drive one. Vince was perfect. He seemed happy in his work, did not question anything or show interest in the business dealing he was facilitating.

Gustav the Pole was not a pedlar of designer drugs. He would have been upset if Vince had ever suggested this. It would be inelegant, lack sophistication, and insult his stylish perfection. It wasn't that Gustav the Pole could get you a dodgy forged document occasionally from his network in the underbelly. Gustav *was* the forger. And a good one at that. The stuff he'd done for Vince was as a favour, as he'd known Kaleena. As a stoic nationalist he did the occasional job to help out a fellow countryman. Meanwhile, the modern age was no longer the cold war, and espionage was not big money these days. However, antiques were, and London was full of them.

Antiques are the 'Emperor's New Clothes' of modern investment. This is much like fashion, where the unflattering nature of an elaborate concoction is far less of an issue as to who the designer was, and whether or not their work is the thing to boast that you're being seen in. Similarly with antiques, you may well have a beautiful Chinese vase from centuries before, but unless you can prove that it was indeed the one once owned by Edward the Seventh and that the dynasty of origin was a particularly good one, then its beauty counts for almost nothing. Therefore, for many antiques, the paperwork is more valuable than the thing itself. They might include a set of receipts that help demonstrate genuine ownership by a celebrity or historic figure, documents that prove authenticity, or the bills of lading to show it came from the place it should have done, and is therefore, probably, genuine. All the paperwork needed to show that the person holding the antique was the rightful owner and therefore had the right to sell it. Antiques and art were an investment. If you wanted something nice to look at then you should buy a poster of a dolphin or a kitten from the greeting card shop. If you wanted to keep your money somewhere other than the banks and away from the taxman, this is how you did it. Not only was

Gustav in the antiques trade, he was one of the few in London that oiled the cogs and made it work. Consequently, his skills and services were highly in demand. As a result, so were the services of Vince the mini-cab driver.

The pitch

Ted Renwick had been courting the ego of Fairchild for long enough, and it was time for him to make his pitch. He'd been carefully feeding Fairchild with the celebrity house-moving enterprise for a few weeks. He'd teased his interest to almost fever pitch, but without ever letting Fairchild get involved. The idea was that, over time, Fairchild would feel completely left out of the most exciting venture ever to be dreamt of. He would jump at the opportunity to get in, and completely forget to ask a number of key questions relating to the authenticity of what was going on.

Ted Renwick and Fairchild sat at the bar whilst yet another charity auction entertained a set of A-list wannabes. Both were drinking dry Martini's, as Ted was selling his special Englishness, and Fairchild was buying into it.

"Thatcher, that was the start of all this!"

Ted launched into his sales pitch, knowing that Fairchild was a soft touch for the common working man, unlike the Iron Lady's reputation.

"Closed mines, took on the unions, sent British Industry packing and let in loads of cheap rubbish from Asia. Not that I have a problem with the Asians mind you. They are bloody good at what they do. But thirty years ago this country made stuff, had a car industry, and now we've gone to the dogs."

Fairchild nodded sympathetically. He'd heard of Thatcher but didn't know much about her. Back in Ohio, UK politics were not a big concern. People knew about the Queen, loved Princess Di's wedding, and were vaguely aware of a 'special relationship' which meant that the British did what the Americans told them to do if somewhere with oil needed invading.

"The Japanese cars are okay but not built to last. In fact, it's quite the opposite. It suits our government to have all the cars fall apart every three or four years just so people have to buy a new one to keep the money circulating. If we had some industries of our own that wouldn't be needed. Look at the classic Jags or even the Mini. Those things kept going for decades. A right bloody waste if you ask me. Notha' Martini, Jono?"

Ted beckoned the bartender a with subtle gesture involving just the middle and index finger of his left hand, the bartender obeyed, demonstrating that Ted was very much the respected man in the room.

"Now American trucks, that's a different matter entirely. Your people know how to make a good solid car. None of this plastic throw-away nonsense. Beautiful machines that last for decades. Look at the Chevy, the Dodge Charger. Proper engineered to last – real American quality. That's what this country is missing. The sooner we get some decent American cars on British roads, things will be different."

Fairchild had been struggling with the thought that the evening's conversation was going to be about British domestic politics of the 1980s. He was in danger of appearing uneducated should he suddenly be expected to contribute to the discussion. However, now they were on American muscle cars and he launched into a reverie about his days as a lad (a lad with a loaded father), of classic cars, of road trips and youth.

For Ted it was like shooting fish in a barrel. Two Martinis later he was ready to make the sale.

"I tell you what Jono, I could triple the money for charity that all the events like tonight make in a week. Once I get the 'Celebs On The Move' up and running, those poor hungry kids'll never want for anything ever again. I just can't get hold of the right trucks over here. Like you say yourself, the only people that can make a good vehicle are the Yanks. I just haven't got the contacts in the states to start exporting trucks from the East Coast to the UK. If I had someone with some real business nouse who could put five or ten good quality trucks on a boat, we'd be laughing. I need someone who has the contacts and abilities to handle all the paperwork. With that, I'd have the thing up and running within six weeks. You've seen for yourself how many of these celebs are up for it."

Fairchild was sold. He offered there and then to join Ted Renwick in the most exciting business venture he'd stumbled across in years. He would use his business links of the East Coast to help buy some great American trucks, and go to the States to arrange everything personally. With his business connections, the trucks would be on a ship heading for UK shores before they knew it. It was perfect. Fairchild, though his charitable gesture would increase the adoration he received from Susan, if that were possible, his reputation in London as the most charitable man in the celebrity social circles would be unquestioned. He might even be able to use the trip to America to deal with some lingering family issues.

Emily

Emily had been fortunate that she was born a girl. Had Fairchild fathered a son and heir, he would have been christened Emiliano, named after his Mexican revolutionary hero. Indeed, Emily had worked out early on in her life that it would be important to distance herself as much as possible from her historic namesake. You didn't get to swan about in the popular group at school and get to be voted as prom-queen if your peers knew you'd been named after a type of moustache. (Of course, in that regard she was just as fortunate that her father's hero wasn't Jose Garibaldi. The choices for the female version of the name are less clear, and people wouldn't be able to work out if she'd been named after either the revolutionary or the biscuit).

Emily's mother had died in a traffic accident on highway 71 when Emily had been just two years old. She had spent her early years growing up in Ohio on their rural estate with her father. However, as she got older, Fairchild worried that Emily lacked the influence of a strong matronly figure to install good womanly values in her. He sent her off to a very expensive all-girls school in New York, where a good education and correct etiquette were the priority. This did have the effect of broadening her horizons, but it was not the reclusive nunnery that Fairchild had imagined it to be. His little girl soon became wise to the modern world, more so than if she'd stayed back on the farm in Ohio.

Inevitably, the father-daughter relationship was a little distant and the pull of life in New York far out-shadowed any desire to return to Ohio. However, the on-going but distant concern from her father was greatly advantageous to Emily in terms of family wealth. This was especially true when it came to renting well-appointed apartments in down-town Manhattan, and financing clothes shopping trips with other girls who had been abandoned in private education by their rich parents. As a result of these many twists of fate, along with the influence of Madonna in her early teens, Emily had not turned out quite as Fairchild had hoped. It was a nineteen-year-old student dressed in a leather jacket and ripped jeans, with a pack of cigarettes in the back pocket that greeted Fairchild at JFK airport. She was not the recreation of her prim mother that Fairchild had thought he'd so heavily invested in. However, his wayward daughter was about to take a gap year. Fairchild saw this as an opportunity. The plan had been hatching in his mind since he had returned from Mexico. Emily should start her gap year in London. He could keep his eye on her, rekindle the father-daughter relationship, and maybe even get her to dress more like a respected Fairchild, and a little less like a rock-chick slut. Maybe along with Susan they'd start to become a sort of family.

Emily also had a plan. However, it was more along the lines of hitting London, whilst being rent free and with easy access to the clubs, bars, and her father's wallet.

The three kings of antiquing

Within two months of starting his new driving career, Vince found that as he was spending so much time driving Gustav the Pole's crew around London, that he didn't actually need to do the mini-cabbing any more. He had basically been paying sixty quid a week for Derek to advertise himself in the yellow pages as a mini-cab firm and then answer the phone before passing on the information to his freelance drivers. Meanwhile, Gustav was finding Vince's driving service incredibly useful. There was a big job coming up in London. Gustav believed it to be the biggest of its kind in years. Consequently, a lot of valuable antiques would suddenly come into the possession of people that they shouldn't do. It was very important that those people had the correct receipts and documents to suggest otherwise, and be able to sell them on quickly.

Making-up or inventing documents of authenticity was not as easy as copying them. Due to the values they represented, they were also documents that would be held to more scrutiny than Vince's pretend Polish driving license. Gustav needed to know exactly which antiques they would have to shift, what the history of those antiques were, and what papers they would have to come with. Once that was known, he needed to know what the original papers and receipts would look like so he could make new ones that demonstrated a slightly different and warped lineage of ownership. To this end he had three of his compatriots working full time on the research.

The three kings of antiquing were Nikolai, Radoslaw and Kaspar. Unlike the brightly-adorned chaps in the nativity, the three of them seemed to dress in long black overcoats, with shabby pin-stripe suits beneath them. The image was set off with stubbly beards and dark sunken bags around their eyes from too many late nights toasting their eastern European roots with cheap vodka.

Nikolai was the main researcher. He was a tall man, but rarely appeared so, as he walked hunched in his dark coat as if constantly battling against heavy rain. He would spend time in dimly lit corners of libraries pouring over obscure dusty volumes, cataloguing antiquities. Often he'd return with heavy moth-eaten books that he would read deep into the night, researching past ownership and sales. The information Nikolai collated enabled him to develop a list of the paperwork that upcoming hot antiques needed to help to cool them back down again.

Radoslaw was a heavy set man who would spend his afternoons visiting antique shops and auctions, occasionally picking up a small trinket on the way. His bargaining skills were enhanced by his gruff menacing tone and lack of vocabulary. It was difficult for frail antique dealers to argue with someone that looked menacing but didn't seem to understand what they said. Later Radoslaw might try to sell that same trinket on to another dealer, usually at a lower price to guarantee the sale. Through this process he gradually established a portfolio of receipts and sales bills with signatures from which Gustav could imitate and reproduce forgeries. As a result of Radoslaws petty dealing, the paper-trail would give Gustav access to the correct size, type and weight of paper that the individual antiques traders used, and have original examples of their signatures and stamps. It was fortunate that the hit list of nouveau rich A-listers did most of their antiquing in London. This was largely due to few of them having a good understanding of antiques and a belief that if they tried to buy them from abroad they would be ripped off by dodgy foreigners and their incomprehensible currency. It was much more reassuring to be ripped off closer to home.

Kaspar was the third and final king. He was a wiry, slightly older man with quick, piercing eyes. He had been in London longer than the rest, and worked as the go-between, linking the forging operation to the heist gang. He would communicate with the boss of the team that would eventually pull off the robbery. The boss-man let him know which members of London's elite were going to be disconnected from their investments, and what those antiques would be.

Between them, they had an efficient and very lucrative business. With the big job coming up, it was Vince's contribution to unwittingly drive the three kings to and from their points of research. This additional work had removed the necessity for the weekly sixty quid investment Vince had needed to make with the mini-cab firm. However, with a regular car load of Polish antiquers, it brought ever closer the investment that the back suspension needed in the FSO Polonez.

The West Coast

Fairchild, almost by default, had a number of business contacts in New York. His father had left him businesses in New York, Cleveland, Buffalo and Pittsburgh. All of which he had generally left to more competent managers in the Fairchild empire to oversee their smooth operation in his absence. Therefore, he decided to call on one of the New York bosses. He knew that they had strong ties with the import-export business, and so he asked him to organize some impressive looking removal trucks, and send them to the Southampton Docks in England.

Following his briefing from Ted Renwick that 'American was best', Fairchild and his employees carried out their research and quickly settled on the ideal choice of furniture remover. They picked out chunky bull-nosed GM trucks, suitable for the wide expanses of the mid-west but probably a little wide and ungainly for the slender back streets of London Town. This was not a consideration of the brief however, so they ordered five of them all in bright orange so that they would stand out and impress quaint English celebrities. That the beasts in question had engines designed for coast-to-coast haulage across the deserts and mountains of the American wilds, was of no concern when this decision was made. The fact that the UK was only 600 miles end to end, or that once you hit the countryside even normal-size vehicles struggled to fit down the windy single lane roads that lead to the manor houses occupied by rock stars squandering their newly found wealth, was of no consequence either. These were the trucks that were built in America and now they were going to strut their bright-orange stuff in the UK as well. That was all that mattered.

A few meetings and handshakes with the right contacts and the trucks were bought, paperwork filed and merchandise loaded onto a freighter bound for England. A week later, Fairchild was on a plane returning to London. Seated next to him, flicking through the in-flight movies and seeing how many miniature bottles of Jack Daniels she could get through during the eight-hour crossing, was Emily.

Driving Kaspar

"Renwick say it must be done 13 June. There no compromising."

Gustav the Pole stared dolefully at Kaspar, Nikolai and Radoslav. They waited patiently for his reaction, which they knew would follow a period of high concentration in his facial expression, followed by a shot of vodka.

Gustav eventually snorted, and then shrugged a little.

"Does he not know these things take time? This is not a cheap magic act, this is an art."

Kaspar had anticipated an emotional response from his temperamental and artistic friend, so continued with his explanation.

"It is the fault of this gullible American who is buying the truck. He want to be first person to be moved by new company. He and English woman stay in apartment near Thames river. He bring his daughter from US and want to make happy family by moving to big house in suburb. He wants daughter be impress by new truck doing their move first."

Kaspar leaned forward and peered at Gustav's sunken dark eyes for a reaction.

"This gives us less than two weeks to find what antiques he has, and make all of the documents."

Kaspar nodded. Renwick had already explained that having quizzed Fairchild and Susan about their possessions, it seemed that most of their London valuables were retained from Susan's first marriage to Alan Ratcliffe. There were a few American civil war items and various vases, silverware, and so forth, but Susan didn't know what they were or anything about their value. For a quick assessment of what they would be stealing, a slight deviation from the normal operating procedures would be required.

"Renwick has persuaded American's woman to have antique valued. Being in the business of moving expensive thing, he make her see he knew about insurance. She thinks that if the antique are valued he get her bargain on insurance. He make appointment for afternoon today."

Vince was summoned from the bedsit apartment on the upper floor, and tasked to drive the three kings to central London.

The suspension squeaked uneasily as they squashed into their positions in the ancient Polish car.

Unusually, Vince's clients were all wearing sunglasses, but otherwise their image was unchanged. Vince was the first to recognise that the British summer in London was never going to be comparable to a day at a Californian beach, but his passengers continued to wear dark overcoats outside of the winter period, which seemed rather strange.

Vince pulled up outside the posh block of flats according to Kaspar's instructions. Well, almost. The brakes seemed to be getting worse, especially with all the weight on board, so in reality they stopped a little further down the street than he had planned.

"We will be one hour. Maybe more. You will wait."

Kaspar issued his brief and clear instructions as the three of them filed off to the entrance to the flats, looking more like a company of undertakers than experts in the antique trade. Of course, they never discussed their business with Vince, but a lot of his driving meant waiting outside auctions and antique shops, so at least he was starting to become more aware of the broad area of their work.

It was quite a warm day, so Vince decided he'd stretch out on the bonnet of the car and catch some rays while he counted the time.

"What the hell is that!?"

Vince opened his eyes, squinting against the sun until he focused on the source of the exclamation. Before him stood an attractive female, a bit younger than him, staring suspiciously at his lime green transport. Vince thought for a moment:

"It's foreign... from Europe."

Vince was giving her enough credit to know it was a car, but beyond that he was unsure where the confusion lay. He assumed from the accent that she was a tourist so decided to convey that he wasn't driving something of national heritage in case she wasted a photo on it.

"Well it sure looks like a big heap of shit."

Vince didn't feel he could argue and decided that perhaps she was more astute than he'd given her credit for. He shrugged to convey his apology for clearly being associated with the eyesore.

"Yaw sound American like. Yam here for a holiday or sommat?"

"Yeah right – holiday. I'm here to stay with my daddy and his god-awful mistress in his go'damn shitty apartment."

"Yaw dow sound like yam enjoying it much?"

Vince's thoughts strayed to his own 'go'damn shitty apartment' and felt that he would happily swap it for the high-class joint he was parked outside right now.

"I've been stuck in this god-awful place for a week. I don't know anyone, the weather stinks, and my daddy is too busy with that floozy to take me out and see stuff, or let me have any fun."

"I could take you out later if you like? I'm not driving many nights these days as most of my work is driving round the Polish antique men."

"So you're the driver that takes around those weird looking guys who just went to our apartment talking antiques with the floozy. I had to get out of there, man. It was like being at a convention of go'damn undertakers!"

The night out

Vince had been very conscious that since Kaleena left he had been missing some key elements from the trade-up scheme. The rules had always been very simple: every three months you trade-up – new job, new girl, new wheels, new pad, new threads, new life. Of course he had his new driving job – which included the 'new wheels', sort of. However, if you counted mini-cabbing and being driver for Gustav as the same occupation as it involved ferrying people about in the same car, then it was also nearly time for a new job trade-up. The other elements of a new life had not even been achieved. Meanwhile, Emily was good-looking, although a little brash, and clearly came from a background of wealth. The very fact he had driven three Poles dressed inappropriately in overcoats to examine the family collection of antiques and heirlooms was testament to that.

That evening, Vince gradually pulled up outside Emily's apartment in his Polish mini-cab. The challenge was that the road sloped downwards and it was a one-way street. In an ideal world he would have approach from the other end so that the up-hill would compensate for the limitation of the brakes. The irony of his recent past life making brake cables did not escape him as he wondered if his former employers might be responsible for his current struggles.

Emily appeared from the apartment entrance. She had requested that Vince did not go up to the apartment so that her father continued to believe she was meeting up with an old school friend from her pseudo-nunnery days. With her barely-there dress and designer jacket, she was clearly ready to hit the town. Fortunately Vince had spent considerable time in the last two and a half months driving party-goes to the most fashionable pubs and clubs the city had to offer. Also, as a result of hanging around in the early hours of the morning, waiting to pick up drunken revellers so they could vomit on his back seat, he also knew a number of the bouncers as well. This made getting into the more exclusive places slightly easier.

After showing Emily a couple of 'real English' pubs, they then went to one of the more popular clubs. To Vince's surprise they'd hit it off straight away. He assumed Emily would be some spoilt brat, which she kind of was, but in a very down to earth way. Clubbing in London was a far cry from the days when he was in the kitchens cleaning up, and listening to the party he was excluded from beyond the other side of the tiled wall. The music pounded and he and Emily danced like exotic birds in a pre-mating ritual. Vince had assumed she would soon spot some strong-jawed, gym-toned Neanderthal and so desert him for something prettier, but not only did she stay with him, they had fun. They were comfortable in each other's company.

At 1.00am, Vince dropped a rather tipsy Emily back outside her apartment. This was the curfew 'daddy' had placed on the school-friend meet-up, and they decided not to get her grounded on her first taste of freedom.

Before she left the car, Emily turned to Vince and gently stroked the side of his face with her hand, before pulling him closer and kissing him.

"What about tomorrow then, handsome?"

Emily's eyes smiled in a way that let Vince know this wasn't just about her next planned escape from the apartment, she really was into him.

"Yeah… alright then."

The hush before the heist

Ted Renwick, as he was known to his partner in business, Jonathan Fairchild, was ready. The trucks, all be them ridiculous monstrosities that didn't fit on any of the roads properly, were in town and ready to go. They were all now fitted with false number plates. Other than the one to be used for Fairchild's place which remained a painful shade of near-luminous orange, Renwick had had the others painted a dull and less conspicuous shade of grubby off-white. Despite his reassurances to the contrary when discussing with their purchaser, their ownership remained in Fairchild's name.

Tomorrow was house moving day. One truck was lined up to move a pop star from her apartment in Islington to the house of her actor fiancé in Notting Hill. Two trucks would move a well know socialite and her millionaire husband from their townhouse in Kensington to a rural retreat in Buckinghamshire, the fourth truck was doing a similar job for an actor in Knightsbridge. Last but no means least, Fairchild was moving from their apartment in Chelsea to a large mansion of a place in Richmond.

For all four customers, the valuable antiques and art had been researched, reviewed, catalogued, had false documents, and in some cases had potential buyers already lined up and waiting.

The ingenious part of the scheme was that all four customers were starting their move from central London locations. The four mobile heist teams would time their house-clearance work so that they departed from their locations an hour after each other. They would then drive to a warehouse that Renwick rented under a different false name, somewhere off the North Circular. They should have approximately an hour to carefully unload each stash of valuables before the next truck arrived to be unloaded. The antiques would be carefully boxed up if necessary. The joy of this being part of a furniture removing scam was that nearly everything of value would have already been carefully boxed up while their owners looked on, and maybe even helped. The antiques that needed shipping immediately, particularly those that would cross over to Europe, would be put in smaller vans and cars. These vehicles were registered to one of Ted Renwick's aliases. However, they were far enough removed from the actual removal of the antiques to be linked to the heist. Drivers would then head for various ferry ports to ensure that the items were out of the country the same day. Other goods would remain in the warehouse and the team would gradually but carefully shift them as buyers and markets became apparent.

The empty trucks, meanwhile, would depart the warehouse in the night and head out to various corners of the country to be abandoned and found by the police some time later.

In principle, it was basically rich people inviting Ted Renwick into their homes, and allowing him to carefully take everything they owned. It was almost too simple.

The incident

Vince had been seeing Emily for about two weeks or more. They had really hit it off. A similar tale of absent parents and a need for self-reliance meant they had a surprising amount in common – even to the extent of socially challenged elderly relatives. Emily genuinely found Vince interesting. She had spent her upbringing in well-to-do circles and with kids from other well-off families. Vince was an entry point to a world where people had little and made do with what they had. It was an existence where real-life struggles had no safety net and you couldn't ask daddy for money when it went wrong. Somehow she respected this. Also, Vince was an honest, uncomplicated person who generally said what he thought, and tried to be kind. This was a refreshing change from the girl-schools and social elite in the Big Apple where social positioning was an art form and genuine trust in your contemporaries was a rarity.

On this particular day, Emily had persuaded Vince to take her sight-seeing in London. Her dad had decided that they were moving to a new place in Richmond in the stupid big truck he'd given some limey business guy for charity. Emily was not impressed. She had come to London to get stuck into the heart and soul of what was going on. She was here for the club scene and the night life, not to disappear into some redundant leafy suburb. Susan Ratcliffe, the new evil stepmother, had been flapping about the big move for days, and so the only logical solution was to get as far out of the way as possible.

Unfortunately, Vince had been called upon to chauffeur for Gustav the Pole during that morning. He had been made to understand that an important meeting had come up and it could not be avoided. The assignation was with one of the high-brow people Kaspar normally met with. This also included delivering a small but quite heavy grey filing cabinet. After waiting outside a posh apartment building for over an hour, Gustav had eventually returned with a heavy looking brief case and no filing cabinet. He then insisted that Vince make a detour to the bank before finally being dropped back at the flat in Whitechapel.

Gustav had spent another thirty minutes in the bank before returning to the car without his briefcase. Subsequently Vince was running very very late.

As he rapidly turned the corner at the top of the road, Vince could see Emily pacing near the gate to the apartment block, looking at her watch. It was too late by the time Vince realised that in his enthusiasm to reach her, his car didn't have the ability to stop outside the front gate. Based on past experience, he would normally end up a few houses further down the hill of the usually quiet and empty back street. However, on this occasion, the plan B parking option was filled with a large and bright orange truck. It wasn't just the brakes that were failing on the Polonez. The steering column had also become a bit temperamental. Often, quite a bit of steering had to take place before the steering rack found a way to respond, and then participate in a change of direction. This occasion was no exception. Despite standing on the brake pedal and steering furiously in a clockwise motion, Vince ploughed the Polonez straight into the back of the shiny new truck.

The car, being fairly heavy and retaining that 70s robust steel-based build, did a surprising amount of damage to the truck. Being much lower than its newly found opponent, the front end of the car had gone a little way under the back of the truck, smashing the truck's bumper, and buckling parts of the area around the right rear wheels.

The removal activities had been started in earnest about an hour before Vince's unfortunate arrival. This meant that there were already quite a number of things stacked up in the removal truck. A few bookshelves and lamps fell over in the back. As they crashed into the sides of the truck they did so with sufficient force to sound like they were inside the drum of a giant steel band. Wooden boxes slid forwards, some teetering on the edge of descent from the end of the truck, some falling straight to the ground. The sound of crockery smashing was amplified impressively as it emanated from the rear of the container and through to the open air. Vince's car, meanwhile, had concertinaed quite a bit, and steam was rushing out of the radiator. The windscreen had shattered, but remained in situ and the windscreen wiper was thrashing backwards and forwards with enthusiasm. From the car's perspective, this was actually a plus, as it had never worked that well before.

The dramatic arrival of Vincent inspired a number of reactions, most of which Vince would never have expected.

Vince looked up and tried to focus at the end of the car, the epicentre of the crash site. Emily was standing next to the car window looking in at him. Rather than appearing shocked, or upset, or even horrified, she was actually grinning at him with a level of childish delight that was usually the reserve of small infants being handed ice-cream at the beach. The evil Susan stepmother had been really grating on her nerves, and Vince smashing into the back of her removal truck was the most entertaining thing to have happened since she arrived in England. It also held almost boundless promise of further entertainment for the rest of the morning.

A little way behind Emily was Susan. The look of shock on her face was so extreme it cracked the heavy make-up round her eyes like the fractured clay of a dried riverbed. This effect multiplied considerably at her realisation that she knew the driver to be her former receptionist.

Vince momentarily shared a similar expression of confused shock. Until that moment, he had yet to work out that the evil step-mother that Emily often referred to was actually Susan Ratcliffe. Emily was new in town, had a strong American accent, and was on a gap year from New York. Susan Ratcliffe, meanwhile, had always lived in London, had a strong London accent, and was not in transit from New York. It should therefore be no great surprise that Vince had failed to link the two. He was, however, able to quickly link the fact that the person whose removal truck he'd just destroyed was the same person whom three months early had lost her hotel in Paddington to an unfortunate chip-pan fire that had started in the kitchens. From her expression, her mood hadn't improved greatly in that time.

The least expected reaction was that of the removal men. One had been carrying a boxed-up set of silverware down the apartment steps when the accident had happened. He had since thrust it into the arms of Susan, and ran over to inspect the damage to the back of the truck. A second removal man had been struggling with the grandfather clock that had been left to Susan by her Uncle Cecil. He left it propping open the apartment door and ran to join the first man in his inspection of the disaster. A third colleague climbed out from inside the truck. He was nursing a headache and a bruised knee from where he'd unexpectedly found himself bouncing into the side of a welsh dresser. The three of them studied the situation. A clear concern was the damage to the rear axle which meant the truck would need some repair before it was properly roadworthy again. A brief argument broke out. Eventually, they all then started to scarper down the hill and vanish round the corner.

As they disappeared from sight, Emily helped to pull open the door of the crumpled car and Vince climbed out.

"Alright there Em? Sorry I'm late."

The police

This was the second time in recent months that Susan Ratcliffe had required the assistance of the Metropolitan Constabulary to investigate the extensive destruction of her property, caused by Vincent Crow. When she had recovered a little from the initial shock of witnessing the crash, she wasted even less time in letting Vince know exactly how she felt about this. Meanwhile, Fairchild had descended from the apartment to find out where everyone had got to. Horrified, he tried to call Renwick on his mobile to let him know what had happened. For some reason, the number that he had no longer worked.

The police arrived quite quickly on the scene. The fact that the removal people had legged-it without at least following the minimum required protocol of exchanging contact information with Vince, seemed to worry them considerably. Their worries increased further when they found that the number plates were no more legally valid than the trucks were. Consequently, having established that the truck was one of a matching set of five, they put out a call for the remaining ones to be rounded up. Within an hour, four of the five trucks had been found, and a number of furnisher removers had been detained for further questioning. Meanwhile, the London flat where Ted Renwick and his wife, Sheila lived, was found to be completely empty, turning out to be the only real example of a successful house-move throughout the whole proceeding.

Fortunately for Gustav the Pole, he had also forged papers and provided receipts to demonstrate that Vince was the legal owner of the FSO Polonez which now had its front end crumpled beneath an American removal truck. At the time that Vince started mini-cabbing, Gustav had astutely decided that in its current state, the car should appear to be held in Vince's name. With all of the car documents along with an M.O.T. to demonstrate roadworthiness registered to Vince, if there was a problem it couldn't be traced back to Gustav. Vince, meanwhile, felt that Derek's Mini-cabs were more likely to retain him if the car he was driving appeared to belong to him. If they'd know, he was only borrowing the dubious vehicle, they might have insisted that he should borrow a slightly better one.

Of course, Vince had no incentive to mention Gustav to the police. It would inevitably bring to their attention his own criminal activity in the use of forged documents. The only thread that could connect them was that Vince was the one who had dropped off the three kings to value the antiques in Susan's apartment. For the moment, only Vince and Emily knew about that, and neither had made the connection.

Compensation

As events unfolded, Fairchild began to realise just how naive and stupid he had been. Somehow he'd been conned by the falsely named 'Ted Renwick' into importing five brand-new getaway trucks from America. To add insult to injury, one of these getaway trucks would be used in the robbery of his own flat, and steal all the worldly possessions of his new found love. This would all have happened beneath his very moustache-clad nose had it not been for Vincent Crow. The only thing to save him from having to live with the embarrassment, and to face the various celebs that had their belongings removed by his trucks, was Vince's disinclination to carry out any meaningful repairs on a borrowed Polish mini-cab.

Eventually, a tow-truck arrived to help the police impound the bull-nosed orange removal truck. The Polonez had been disentangled from the trucks rear and then dragged to the side of the road and abandoned there. Clearly the police didn't link this vehicle to the criminal gang and so abandoned it with the view that it was Vince's problem. Having taken statements, finally the police and C.I.D. had left. The Fairchilds, Susan and Vince remained sitting on the steps to the apartment. Fairchild was the first to break the silence:

"It's funny how things turn out, Vince, but I guess I really should be thanking you for crashing into the truck. You've saved me a lot of embarrassment in the long run, and in your own way, you've kinda saved the day."

Susan shot Vince a cold and sour look. Her experience of him was the ability to do the opposite of saving the day. Of course, the Armstrong Hotel burning down had worked out well for her. So had the car crash, in the sense that he'd only destroyed a limited percentage of her worldly possessions and prevented the rest from being stolen. However, just because there are positive spin-offs from someone doing considerable damage to your property, it doesn't mean you have to like them for it.

"Well, it's nice of you to say so, Mr Fairchild. Of course the car's a write-off, and it's only covered third-party. So this means I've lost me mini-cabbing job. Have yaw got any jobs going?"

Emily was sitting next to him, holding his hand. She decided that now was a good time to pitch in with her own confession. Many aspects of Emily's recent deceptions regarding her London social life had paled into insignificance following the dramatic accident. These were watered down further by the arrival of the police, the later arrival of C.I.D., and the eventual uncovering of an international smuggling ring. Emily recognised this as a good time to come clean about the deception, and explain to her father that she'd not been hanging out with an old school friend. Vince was her current distraction. Fairchild was indeed very distracted by the chaos he had been involved in and had partial caused. For Emily, it had turned out to be a very sound judgement.

Fairchild considered what he had learned. The young man who had just saved the day was also a good friend of his daughter. He seemed to be a guy who was honest, prepared to work for a living, and Emily liked him. He might turn out to be a good influence on her. Not only that, he was looking for a job.

"Gee, Vince. There's bound to be some kind of job I can find for you. I'm gonna need a driver myself once we head out to Richmond and live in the suburbs. Hell, I'm gonna need a car as well. How would you feel about coming to work for me as a chauffeur? The new place has servant quarters at the rear of the building so you can stay there if you need to. You and Emily would need to go and pick out a new car first, of course."

Fairchild beamed at his daughter. There was nothing that said 'I want to mend our father daughter relationship' better than 'here's a blank check, go and pick out a car.'

Susan's look managed to become even more sour, and even more shooting. Emily beamed with delight. Vince just looked confused, trying to take everything in. This morning he had crashed an old bomb into a removal truck, damaging several pieces of valuable furniture, whilst secretly picking up the daughter of a rich American to avoid his inevitable disapproval. As a result, he was being invited into the household with the offer of a job as a driver in compensation for his troubles. It just went to show that the trade-up theory really did work. If you put yourself out there enough, eventually something would come of it.

When Vince returned to Whitechapel that evening to pick up his few possessions and clothes, he couldn't help but notice that Gustav had cleared out of the building as well. The three kings were also noticeable by their absence. Vince shrugged. At least it saved him having to explain to them what had happened to their car.

Chapter 5 – Chauffeur

The wheels

Vince had never bought a new car before. In fact he'd never bought a car before. This was strongly attributable to the insufficient funds generated by cleaning pub kitchens, and also that he'd never passed a driving test.

For Emily meanwhile, shopping, especially for expensive things, was a well-honed talent.

It was a fairly brief conversation before they both concluded that the family saloon run-around needed to be a Porsche Cabriolet. The facts pointed to nothing else: money was not an issue; Vince had once had a poster of a big red Porsche on his wall as a kid; Emily needed something cool and European, and where the roof came down as this was essential for looking cool on road trips. Photos of her in anything less would not be acceptable with the girls back in New York.

The showroom owner had immediately looked down his nose at Vince as he sauntered in and started gazing in awe at the expensive motors. However, he quickly 'looked up his nose' (if indeed that is the inverse of his reaction to Vince) as Emily produced the snazzy shimmering credit card her daddy had given her to make the purchase. Within an hour they were rolling out of the showroom in a bright red Porsche. The experience was a total contrast to Vince's former ride in every way – particularly the brakes, as he discovered when they kangaroo-ed their way back to the Richmond suburbs.

For Vince, trade-up number four had started sensationally well. Bearing in mind that the trade-up requirements were the job, the girl, the wheels, the pad and the threads, this one was coming good in most regards:

The Job – Emily had helped negotiate a healthy salary based on the need for her boyfriend to be able to keep her in the clubs and restaurants she wanted to be accustomed to. It was at least five times what he'd been able to make when he was mini-cabbing, and that was still more than Susan Ratcliffe had been prepared to part with at the hotel.

The Wheels – A red Porsche. From a trade-up perspective he'd actually reached the top. The only higher you could reach from driving such a car was actually owning one. However, as he was now practically family, this was a minor detail. Also, in the absence of a driving licence, it was probably better that the car was registered to Fairchild and the insurance was fully comprehensive and 'any driver'.

The Girl – Emily. She was good-looking, fun to be with, rich, and she liked him. Her accent was difficult to pick up at times though, a bit like a foreign language. It made him wonder how rock-stars, the likes of Ozzy Ozborne got on when they permanently moved to the states. If he ended up marrying her and had to live in New York or something, he would have to try to really tune in. Maybe he'd have lessons like when they had to listen to those scratchy tapes of people talking in French in classes at school. However, apart from the language barrier, what more could you ask for?

The Pad – Richmond townhouse servant quarters. The servants' quarters allocated to him were bigger than the small terrace house he previously shared with his nan. It was much nicer and cleaner too. In contrast to the dishevelled 1960s time-machine back in the Midlands, most of the stuff inside the servants quarters actually worked like it was supposed to. The washing machine washed, the toaster toasted, little things like that. For Vince, this was comparable to winning the lottery.

The Threads – Okay, so nothing was ever perfect.

Driving the Fairchilds

Chauffeuring was the first job for Vince where a formal hat was demanded. That and the ridiculous tunic with brass buttons made him feel like something out of an Agatha Christie novel. He half expected to be invited to the drawing room to answer difficult and leading questions from an elderly Belgian. Tragically, a 1930's costume drama was the quaint look Fairchild was going for, as it would match his out-dated fairy tale vision of what fannying around with the English upper-crust should involve. Vince was just lucky he wasn't being cajoled into a coachman's outfit, with riding boots, tails and powdered wigs.

Despite his high society ambitions, Fairchild was currently keeping a low profile in London. Following his social embarrassment with the antiques con, involving various celebrities and high society members, he'd made a conscious effort to turn his much needed attention to his newly assembled family. After all, Susan and he needed to settle into their new home, and make Emily feel as welcome as possible. As a result of this nesting period, Vince found that there wasn't a high demand for his driving services from his new employer.

The need to be transported by Vince was similarly under-required by Susan. She wanted nothing to do with Vince at all. Firstly, he had extensively damaged her Paddington hotel. He had since reappeared in her life, only to randomly smash up various family heirlooms. However, it was more the fact that he held considerable knowledge about the underhand and slightly unethical way she had run the hotel and employed people in a rather exploitative way that concerned her. This was not a topic she needed to come up between her and Vince. Especially when Fairchild was in earshot.

This meant that for the first two weeks as a chauffeur, Vince was mainly on call to drive Emily around, which usually involved taking her out in London. However, the time would come soon enough when this would all change.

Fairchild's plan had been to have Emily and Susan living in the same house and bonding. In American popular culture, all TV families have various day to day social and personal issues to overcome. However, they all live in big houses in suburbia with a lovable paternal father to hold the family together, whilst doing DIY in a big woollen jumper. A few heart to hearts and some awkward but mildly humorous events later, and the strength of the family bond is shored up sufficiently to enable them to put together a clips show about it. This was very much the plan that Fairchild was trying to instigate. However, it was clear that the only bonding going on was between Vince and Emily in the servants' quarters. He, Susan and Emily barely spent any time together as a family. There needed to be a radical change.

As always, Fairchild looked to his hero Zapata for inspiration. What was it about him that had inspired the residents of the village of Anenecuilco, where Zapata was born, to elect Zapata to be president of the village's defence committee, and fight for the village's rights against the Hacienderos? Was it that he looked handsome in a cowboy outfit, or that he had a well-groomed upper lip? Was it that he'd been a courageous and dutiful soldier, a natural leader, or that he was famed as a skilled horseman and bullfighter? Fairchild quickly concluded that it was most likely to be the whole thing with the horses and the cowboy outfit that had won the hearts of his people and given him such popularity. Horses were such beautiful and inspiring animals. A person who had such respect and love for these creatures would also inspire love and respect themselves. The solution to forge a meaningful path for his disjointed family was going have to be an equestrian one.

They were going to have to pull together. Despite their many differences and needs, they would somehow all have to get interested in horses. Aware that none of his recently assembled family was in anyway acquainted with horses, he concluded that they should probably start with small ones. It was for this reason that Fairchild gathered his family and Vince to the drawing room on a Saturday afternoon. To Vince, this very much resembled a scene from a play where key characters had been assembled to discuss an unexplained murder, a fact to which Vince's tunic-based outfit contributed significantly. Fairchild announced that they would be departing the following Monday on a pony trekking adventure.

Susan, at first, was horrified. She was not an outdoors person. If she was going to bond with someone else's adolescent spoilt brat, it needed to be over something civilised, like choosing the colour of upholstery, or preparing a soufflé. Not being exposed to the elements in a damp field on a big sweaty horse. Moreover, horsey-type people were not a set that had ever appealed to Susan. They usually talked like they had a plum in their mouth, had uncouth verbal exchanges about cleaning filth from stables – an element of the horsey thing in which they seemed to revel, in an atmosphere that invariably hummed of damp animal. She was all the more horrified when she found that Vince would be the one to drive them there.

Emily was delighted with the plan, and said so. Fairchild was, then, also delighted – so one-nil to Emily. Of course she had no intention of bonding with Susan Ratcliffe. The permed cockney nightmare was never going to replace her mother and it wasn't like she was looking to fill the gap anyway. However, it might be fun to go on a bit of an adventure into the wilds with Vince tagging along. A few days break from the monotony of clubbing and drinking might not be such a bad thing. If they could get away from the elderly ones, then it could even develop the essence of a proper road trip.

Journey

Fairchild had long been under the impression that Britain was a nation of four seasons. It was very clear in all the relevant literature that this extended to three months of winter, followed by three months each of spring, summer and autumn. (In fact he'd understood it to be winter, spring, summer and 'fall'. However, despite this inaccuracy, the point of note is that his planning was based on using the four-season system). He had not been sufficiently astute to realise that this regimented system did not apply to the mountains of North Wales.

When Vince had helped pick out the red Porsche, he had not been particularly astute either. Whilst it looked, and indeed was, cool to drive to London clubs in with a cute Yankee chick in the passenger seat, it was clearly not the vehicle of choice for a pioneering Anglo-American family holiday up a welsh mountain. There was very little room in the back the car, which meant that Fairchild had to sit up front with Vince, with the two women squashed uncomfortably in the back. With the car's engine also being located in the back, and Susan's make-up and toiletries squeezed into the space that represented a boot at the front of the car, the remaining bags and clothing were also jammed into any remaining space between legs and on laps.

Caught between a rock and a hard place, Susan had decided the foldable roof of the car had to remain securely in place, as her perm would recover better from being squashed against it rather than being windswept all the way up the M4. This limited the available room further. Eventually the family started their journey to Wales in an uncomfortable car, in an uncomfortable silence, and with a number of very uncomfortable passengers.

Even though there was a lack of space and extra weight, Vince had been looking forward to the drive, and enjoyed the first stint that morning as he sped up the motorway. Despite the weight in the car, the Porsche was still an incredible thing to drive. Especially if your more recent driving experiences were limited to being a mini-cab driver in a Polonez with limited braking capacity. However, once they'd crossed the bridge into Wales and started heading north, the appeal of driving the Porsche was quickly lost.

The rains started, and the world looked damp, grey, and cold. The roads were windy and small, and Fairchild was not the best at following a map. Their damp lunch time stop, somewhere in the Brecon Beacons, did not inspire the uncomfortable silence to ease greatly. A limp egg sandwich and a cup of chewy coffee from an urn in the café, failed to inspire the adventurers on their way.

Some further poor map reading, combined with the limited vision as the dark clouds poured their rains onto the mountains of Snowdonia, were largely responsible for their late arrival. Vince grounding the low-slung Porsche on a large rock on the track leading up to Pony Trekking stables and guesthouse, didn't help. Especially when they all had to get out to reduce the weight inside the car and see if it would lift up enough to be able to get it free. Susan was particularly annoyed at the suggestion that her bulk was a significant contribution to the poor clearance of the car, and her annoyance was magnified considerably once she'd climbed out and her hair got wet.

It was a drenched, bedraggled crew that walked the final 400 yards through the stair-rods that evening before knocking on the door of the 'Nebria Nivalis Pony Trekking Centre.' Susan was least happy, but Emily had gone into a big sulk as well. This was not the care-free, fun-filled road trip she could share tales of with the girls back in college.

The stables

The early morning sunlight blazed through the thin curtains of the dormer windows and announced that a new day, filled with promise, had arrived. Fairchild found some renewed energy, was inspired to make an early start and took a quick shower before waking Susan from her slumbers. Vince was already up. He was enlisting the help of the woman that ran the place to solve his grounded car problem. As promised the previous evening, she used her tractor to help lift the Porsche from where it had run aground in the storm, so that Vince could drive it the short distance to the farmyard.

'Nebria Nivalis Pony Trekking Centre' was owned by Dr. Daniel Sutton and his slightly eccentric wife, Judy. He was a retired university lecturer, and Dr. Sutton considered himself as one of the top ten authorities on beetles in the British Isles. On retirement he decided to dedicate his remaining years to his lifelong passion, and moved to Snowdonia to study, monitor and record the goings on of the Snowdon 'rainbow' beetle. It was a life dedicated to crawling around in the acidic grasslands above the treelines of the Welsh mountains and getting scientific about small black insects. For this he needed a base, and eventually he purchased an old farmhouse on the slopes of a mountain pass, so that each morning he could doggedly trudge up the slopes to visit his studies. In fact he would stay out for days at a time, and Judy became very used to him being missing for up to a week without feeling the urge to call a rescue team.

Meanwhile, Judy had converted the farmhouse stables into a pony trekking centre to keep herself entertained. The business had been a success, with many visitors assuming they were coming to something with a Welsh name that they didn't understand, but in fact they were visiting stables named after a genus of locally resident but nether-the-less rare beetle. The naming of the trusty steeds under Judy's care took a similar vein to the method for labelling the stables. This was very much to the disappointment of the young girls escaping from the urban gloom on their exciting holiday to the wilds of Snowdonia. They expected their ponies to have special titles that would be equally fitting for unicorns: names like Princess, Shadow, or Starburst. This was very much not the case. The fact that people were not only getting to ride a horse but were also being indirectly educated about beetles was rarely appreciated by the customers. It was always a considerable disappointment to Dr. Sutton and so he tried to have as limited interaction with the guests as possible.

After a hearty English breakfast, reminiscent to some in the party of the grease-soaked fare of the Armstrong Hotel in Paddington, before it had been accidentally gutted by fire, Judy invited her guests to wait in the courtyard whilst she readied the horses.

The group milled about outside, looking at rusty and obsolete bits of tractor accessory. All farms seemed to have a corner or open shed with piles of brown and crusty tools and attachments from the early 20th century, and the 'Nebria Nivalis Pony Trekking Centre' was no exception. Eventually Judy led a collection of nags from the stables and introduced them to the Fairchilds.

The first mount to arrive from the depths of the aging barn was for Fairchild. It was a chestnut-coloured horse called Cardinal. In the absence of Dr. Sutton, Judy had explained the beetle thing over breakfast, and added to this by inviting them to refer to the beetle photographs displayed on the wall in the reception. (They were informed that Dr. Sutton on his return would happily present his collection of slides if they were interested, but the Fairchilds had wisely declined).

Susan was next to receive her horse, a large black beast named Death-Watch. Emily was given a dappled pony called Green-Tiger, and finally, Vince was presented with a brown horse called Cockchafer. Meanwhile Sexton, Stag, Minotaur and Longhorn all remained confined to their stables. The Sutton's formative years were clearly in a well-mannered age, where double-entendres were for a generation of teenagers that had yet to be invented.

The first challenge of the morning was getting on to the back of the noble steeds in order to ride them. Emily had ridden a horse or two in the summer holidays when visiting horsey-type friends in up-state New York, and quickly alighted Green-Tiger and patted her neck. Green-Tiger gave a gentle bray in appreciation that it was clearly her turn to get the tourist who knew which was the front end of a horse. Emily, meanwhile, was aware that a good relationship between rider and horse was vital if you didn't what to get thrown off or kicked.

Susan's ample yet un-athletic frame may well have had attributes that ensnared Fairchild. However, when it came to ascending the beast that was Death-Watch, she couldn't actually raise her leg as high as the stirrup.

"Vince, come over and give me a leg up!"

Susan glared at Vince until he passed his horsed reins to Emily and went over to help.

"Alright there, Mrs Ratcliffe. It's quite big horse when you look at it."

It was an even bigger horse if you had to get on it. From Emily's perspective it was a most entertaining start to the morning and she decided that perhaps the trip was looking up after all. It finally took a shoulder from Vince beneath the posterior of his former employer, as well as Fairchild pulling from the other side, to get Susan on top of her mount. This was the least dignified arrival on top of a horse ever experienced by Death-Watch and his compatriots. Death-Watch whinnied at the realisation he'd drawn the shortest ever straw, and received a sympathetic look from Green-Tiger. Susan, who was aware that she mustn't loose her temper with Emily's giggles, shot a piercing glare at Vince instead.

When, eventually, all of the clan were successfully perched on top of a horse, they walked out to the paddock for the first lesson: 'walking around a bit in a circle'. Of course the horses all knew the routine and so there was little controlling needed from their riders. After a while they had to learn to trot. This required participants to develop a posture that meant that both rider and mount moved gracefully along as one. For Susan, this proved to be an even less-dignified manoeuvre than getting on the horse had been.

Fairchild's mood was much improved as the morning went on. He decided that his scheme was proving to have an element of success. Emily, if not bonding with Susan, was at least entertained by her. Finally they were doing things together as a family.

After an hour or so it was time for a break. Susan not so much dismounted Death-Watch as tumbled from him, whilst holding the reins to steady herself. In the process her leg swung out as it finally unhooked from the stirrup, and connected forcefully with the side of Cardinal. Cardinal's understated response was to steady himself and take a step sideways. It was unfortunate that this step meant that his iron shoe-clad hoof and most of his weight ended up on the foot of Fairchild, who was standing on the other side.

Fairchild was not expecting this, and it took him a while to persuade Cardinal to address the situation and move his hoof away to another part of the mountain that wasn't already being used. Once Cardinal had complied with the request, Fairchild's reaction became rather less dignified. Hopping and swearing quickly deteriorated to sitting and moaning.

After a degree of calm had been achieved, and Judy had rattled off a string of soothing anecdotes about similar but far worse horse-based mishaps, Vince helped Fairchild back to the guesthouse. Judy treated his swollen foot with some cream and the others watched as it continued to swell and turn various shades of blue and black. Emily and Vince left Judy and Susan to competitively coo over their patient and returned to the paddock.

"Yaw seem quite good at this horse stuff."

Emily patted Green-Tiger, and then went over to pat Death-Watch, and offer him a handful of hay. After all, he had been the star of the morning and deserved a show of gratitude.

"I guess so. Hopefully, Daddy will rest up and that god-awful woman will stay with him. We can go off on a romantic horse ride across the mountains."

Emily looked wistfully at the horizon. A romantic gallop across the untamed wilderness, like something from the King Arthur legends, was a better story than some naff road-trip. Vince also looked forward to the immediate future. He was not a country person. However, his accumulated knowledge about dampness, muddiness, and the British weather in general, meant that he did not quite share the fanciful dreams of his girlfriend.

Trekking

Three key decisions were made. All of them without Vince's input. (He was, after all, a 1930's style chauffeur and therefore not required to participate in household management affairs. To Vince it seemed a little unfair that he was expected to pony trek – which was quite a stretch to his job description, but yet not encouraged to voice an opinion on it.)

The first decision made by the upper management was that Fairchild was to go to see the local doctor, in case his foot was broken. The small rural surgery of Dr. Gwyneth Jones was two villages away down the valley. Having declined the option of being carried there in the mechanical bucket on the front to Judy's tractor, it was agreed that Fairchild would get there by Porsche.

The second decision was that Judy, owner of the stables and not Fairchild's official chauffeur, would drive him. The reason for this was linked to the third decision. Fairchild had insisted that Susan, Emily and Vince spend the afternoon trekking up the mountain on badly named ponies as per the original plan. Fairchild wanted to make sure that his misfortunate coming together with Cardinal did not stop the others from enjoying their quality time together. This was explained to the group in very much the style of someone who was on their death bed, croaking out their final words in-between spitting up clods of blood, rather than just a bloke whose foot had been temporarily stuck under a horse. Fairchild role-played his final moments of life, and was dramatically using up his imagined last breaths available to dish out his final wishes to loved ones.

An early lunch was hastily arranged, after which Judy and Vince managed to get Susan back onto Death-Watch. Fairchild watched from the passenger seat of the car.

The three remaining pony trekkers set out, up the stony track and in to uncharted territory. As they left the stables, the valleys echoed to the sound of Judy roaring down the lane at immense speed, as pebbles and small stones scattered in all directions. The chances of the Porsche getting grounded on a large rock a second time with that kind of momentum was unlikely to say the least.

Emily and Green-Tiger led the way up the hill, followed by Vince and then by Susan on their respective mounts. Death-Watch, whilst having accepted his unfortunate fate for the week, had decided to at least try to enjoy himself and stopped to eat as much hedgerow clover as he could at every opportunity. This was much to Susan's frustration but she lacked the horseman skills to do very much about it.

After a couple of hours of climbing the mountain, negotiating valleys and rocky outcrops as they did so, they reached the start of a flatter moorland area. To their left the endless rocky slopes continued, but behind them the view of Snowdonia was breath-taking.

Emily and Green-Tiger stopped, Vince and Cockchafer came alongside to join them. Together they waited to let Susan catch up. She was nowhere in sight.

"I wasn't so sure about this go'damn trip, but the view is breath-taking from up here."

Emily reached over and held hands with Vince.

"Yaw can see for miles. I bet yaw could see Wolverhampton from up here if you knew which direction to be looking in."

Emily nodded. She had no idea what Wolverhampton was, but suspected its presence in this idyllic view might detract from the wild and untamed splendour of the scenery.

Back down the track, Death-Watch had found a juicy clump of buttercups. Buttercups were his favourite. He was rather surprised that Cockchafer had missed such a magnificent crop as he'd been ahead and must have passed by them as well. It had been a tough day, but finally his luck was changing for the better. For the umpteenth time, he absently bent forward and started to graze, loudly grating his teeth as he did so, trying to drag out the sensation of fresh buttercups for as long as possible. Susan, for the umpteenth time, got steadily more frustrated.

"Come on you bloody animal! If you think I've come all the way up this mountain only to get left behind by those two brats while you gorge yourself, you've got another thing coming!"

With that, she didn't gently kick her horse in the side, as instructed by Judy, she fully walloped her chubby heels deep into his gut. The result was surprising to both.

Death-Watch set off up the hill at a full and spritely gallop. Susan just about managed to join him in this whilst clinging to his neck, but was largely present because her foot was stuck in the left stirrup. Just before reaching Emily and Vince, Death-Watch finally freed himself from the hefty burden that had ruined his buttercup patch, and continued past the others to indulge in a pleasurable and solo gallop across the moorland.

Vince and Emily immediately dismounted from their horses and rushed over to where Susan had thudded into the gorse. Emily took her hand whilst Vince tried to help her sit up. She glared into his eyes with a venom unlike any look she had dealt out before. This was quite an achievement, as she'd been practicing a lot recently.

"This is all your fault! I will see you pay for this, Vincent!"

Just as she spat out her threatening prophecy, there was a loud and deep rumble of thunder. Vince assumed this was linked to the evil way Susan had biblically delivered her words, and a shiver ran down his spine.

The mountain

The thunderclap had also surprised the horses. However, all three of them were already galloping happily across the moorland and so they thought no more of it. Death-Watch had inspired this fun event. Clearly an invigorating gallop over the moors was far preferable to lugging those awful townies up and down the mountain on such a pleasant afternoon, so Green-Tiger and Cockchafer had immediately decided to join in as well.

Vince, having replaced Susan on the ground to stew over all the problems in her life, stared out across the moorland. It seemed that their side of the mountain had beautifully clear weather, and may well hold the promise of a glimpse of the West Midlands, if you could work out which direction you were facing. However, just around the other side of the mountain, the drizzle-soaked fog was quickly rising and would soon be closing in. Vince watched the horses as they disappeared over the horizon. As he did so, he noticed the first tentacles of the mist as it clawed its way around the crags and outcrops of the lower slopes and purposely crept ever closer.

"The mists seem to be rising, Emily. Those horses are long gone. We should probably start to make our way back to the stables."

"You're not bloody-well going anywhere, Vincent."

Susan added a slight agonising groan to the end of her statement to add emphasis. Vincent recalled her recent threatening behaviour, and shuddered a little. He decided not to pursue his current line of advice further.

"A person with a damaged back should not be moved until the paramedics arrive. And you're not leaving me like this on my own up here. God knows what's creeping around out there in the wilderness. Wolves, snakes, murderers, rapists!"

Based on their current experience, a couple of small birds and three annoyingly absent horses were all that Vince believed to make up the unknown terrors of their immediate environment. However, he knew better than to argue, so he looked to Emily for support.

"Vince has a point. The mist is really starting to come up the mountain. The most sensible thing to do is get back before we're completely lost out here."

The mist

It felt like they had been lost on the moors for hours. The three of them huddled together for warmth against a rock, near to where Susan and Death-Watch had finally become disconnected. The fog had indeed risen quickly, and together, Emily and Vince had carried Susan very carefully and noisily to where a nearby large rock rose from the moorland. There was a slight cleft to offer shelter from the wind. However, in reality, this provided little advantage. The peril at hand was the dense drizzly fog that encompassed the mountain side, soaked through their thin summer clothes and hid all possible landmarks that would have saved them from total disorientation. This situation did not improve a couple of hours later when the moonless night began to draw in. The grey swirling gloom became a black, impenetrable and damp void.

Vince continued to wonder how Susan expected the paramedics and air ambulance to arrive if no one had actually alerted the emergency services in the first place. Susan meanwhile, with an edge of hysteria to her voice, kept muttering about how Fairchild would see they hadn't returned and would send out the search parties. Vince was not totally sold on this theory. Apart from anything else, how would they know where to look? No one but themselves knew the route they had taken, and it was not like they were visible in the black night's foggy gloom.

Vince was right to doubt that Fairchild was currently coordinating the deployment of a substantial search-and-rescue mission across the breadth of Snowdonia. In fact, he was in a local tavern two villages down the road from the pony trekking centre. He was buying drinks for any locals that were prepared to listen to him drone on, as long as he kept getting the beers in. To all intents and purposes, he was having a lovely time. In fact, his holiday had really picked up ever since his horse landed on his foot.

This is the real England he thought to himself, despite being in Wales. (Geography wasn't his strong suit and he assumed that anything between the East Coast of America and the start of France counted. To Fairchild, 'Britain', 'United Kingdom',

'England' and 'Scotland', were all synonyms of the same place, presumably developed to help out poets like Shakespeare when they were trying to get things to rhyme. 'Wales' he'd not even heard of until he'd been expected to read the map on the way there.)

Anyway, he was spending his evening in a cosy, low-roofed, dimly lit bar, filled with ale jugs and genuine memorabilia of days that were long since gone by. Mismatching furniture fashioned from ancient wood cluttered the small rooms, deliciously polished by centuries of story tellers taking their turns to take the weight off their feet and spin a yarn or two. Tonight was his turn to be that minstrel and entertain his brothers across the ocean.

"Get another round in please."

Fairchild called out his instruction to the barman, and the five or six men gathered around the bar muttered various noises to indicate their gratitude. Fairchild had entertained them all with his pony trekking story and wondered what topic to engage them with next. He decided that perhaps they'd enjoy hearing about Zapata the Mexican Revolutionary. He would certainly enjoy telling them.

Dr. Gwyneth Jones had not been available on the arrival of Fairchild and Judy at her surgery. She had been out on call, assisting a local sheep farmer with a rather delicate injury which her oaths of confidentiality prevented her from divulging. She had only returned at seven that evening. Having agreed to examine his foot, she judged Fairchild's injury as heavy bruising but no breaks, bandaged him up, and gave out some pain killers to stop the whinging. Due to the late hour, the difficult roads, and Judy driving the Porsche in very much the same way she drove a tractor, Fairchild decided the gear box would be safer if they found rooms at the local inn for the night. They would return first thing in the morning. The pain killers were now mixing very gregariously with the local bitter, as demonstrated by the flush to Fairchild's cheeks.

***

Despite the cold and the damp, Vince had actually managed to drift off to sleep on his rocky pillow. He was therefore shocked when woken suddenly by a frantic Susan Ratcliffe, not only with renewed mobility, but actually sitting on his chest shaking him awake.

"Vince, there's an evil spirit rising from the dead!"

Vince tried to sit up, to find he was literally face to face with Susan. He knew this from her warm breath, her pounding heart and heaving and quaking other bits crushed against him. The night, of course, was still moonless and foggy, and as dark and damp as wearing a blind fold in a carwash with the windows open.

"Am yaw sure? It's very dark and misty out there."

By this stage Emily was awake and had reached out to Vince beside her to see what was happening.

"What the hell's goin on?!"

Her sense of touch indicated to her that her new pseudo step-mother and current boyfriend were locked in an incredibly intimate embrace against the neighbouring rock.

"He rose up out of the mist, groaning and wailing!"

Susan's husky voice quivered uncontrollably.

"Vince! What the hell were you thinking?!"

Emily's shock in believing that Vince had instigated the entwined nature of him and the step-mother, was matched only by Vince's innocence in not realising what she had concluded.

"I couldn't move or get away. It was like I was paralyzed by the force of his presence upon me!"

"Vince!"

"It's probably just a bad dream, Mrs Ratcliffe."

For Susan, this seemed to be the final straw of her imminent breakdown. She wrapped her arms around Vince and buried her head between his neck and shoulder and wept.

"Hold me Vince. I need you!"

Vince held her as instructed. Emily meanwhile would have stormed off in fury, if she could have seen where to storm to. Instead she decided she would remain and silently exude fury in the direction of Vince instead.

Ghost

As all students of the beetle genus *Nebria* will be well aware, the Snowdon 'Rainbow' Beetle is one of the many variations of ground beetle to be found in the British Isles. As a ground beetle, it is therefore habitually nocturnal. This means if a scientist is to become fully acquainted with the goings on, or even goings off, of these small industrious chaps, they must adapt their ways and become somewhat nocturnal themselves. As a result, it was not unusual for Dr. Sutton to spend his nights crawling around on his hands and knees in the Welsh highlands with a head torch strapped to his overly-large cranium, following the adventures of beetles as they diligently hunted for prey amongst the dewy moorland grasses. This had become a nightly routine for Sutton over recent years. He would become so engrossed in his pursuit he'd spend whole nights on the mountains, damp-knee-ed and muddy, with no sense of time, or direction. In the morning he would often be surprised to find himself up to two kilometres from where he had started out on his night-crawl, so engrossed he was in his beetle soap-operas. This spiritual absence from reality neither worried nor concerned him. The various authorities that received reported sightings of a possible escapee from an asylum gradually stopped paying attention as well.

It was in a dense and damp fog at one o'clock in the morning when Dr. Sutton, on a routine crawl, happened to shuffle past the lost pony trekkers: Vince, Susan and Emily. The glow of the head-torch half a foot from the ground was the light that had originally alerted Susan Ratcliffe to an additional presence on their mountain side. Sutton was fairly elderly, and his rheumatism was not benefiting from his particular choice of exercise. Having unknowingly passed-by the group by several metres, his joints demanded a short break and a stretch. He righted himself on his knees stood up for a moment, and extended his arms out. He then exhaled a long and wistful groan, as his aging back creaked into place. This pain-releasing methodology completed, he returned to his knees refreshed, and crawled on. Within moments he would disappear out of sight behind the next rock, of which Snowdonia was not in short supply, and continue his beetle observations. To Susan, the light that suddenly appeared in the mist had rapidly turned into the silhouette of a man rising from the ground through the mists, reaching for her, and moaning before disappearing back to the depths of the earth.

Of course, when Susan eventually pounced on Vince and raised the alarm, Sutton was long gone. Physically, he was only about twenty metres away behind the next rock, but relatively speaking, as he was a little hard of hearing, and had just found a particularly fine specimen of a Violet Ground Beetle, he might as well have been on the moon.

Morning

Vince was first to wake as the early rays of morning light ventured over the horizon and began to slowly burn away the remnants of the night's mist.

It had been a difficult night. Vince had eventually dislodged the distraught Mrs Ratcliffe from where she had mounted him, and eased her on to the ground beside him. Her emotional exhaustion meant that she slept quite soon afterwards. It was during this process that Vince realised that Emily was no longer on speaking terms with him, but he couldn't work out why – particularly as she wouldn't speak to him to tell him why she wasn't speaking to him.

As both Susan and Emily were both fast asleep, Vince decided he would abandon them in their peaceful slumber and head down the mountain side to get help. Meeting up with Fairchild and helping him to rescue his family was preferable to facing two frenzied women when they finally woke. With the decision made, he headed back down the track that they had come up, past the buttercup patch which had caused all the problems in the first place.

An hour and a half later, Vince arrived in the stable yard. It was not too difficult to find the way back, as after a while he could see the stables in the distance to get his bearings. Finding the exact route they'd used through the gorse and rocky outcrops was then less important. Having wandered into the farmyard, he noted that he was not the first returnee. Death-Watch, Green-Tiger and Cockchafer had clearly all made it back a long time before, and were happily munching into a pile of hay by the stable doors. As he walked around to the guesthouse, he noticed the red Porsche was returning cautiously up the farm track.

"Mornin', Mr Fairchild. Yaw foot's better then?"

Fairchild climbed out of the driver's seat and then walked with a slight hobble to the other side of the car to open the door for Judy and assist her in removing her robust frame from the low bucket-seat on the passenger side.

"Nothing broken, luckily. The swelling's going down. Should be completely fine by tomorrow. Where are the girls?"

"Mrs Ratcliffe fell off of her horse, and didn't want to be moved. She seems a lot better now though. Anyway, we lost the horses and spent the night on the mountain, what with Mrs Ratcliffe and the fog and everything, but now I've come back early to fetch some help."

Fairchild looked horrified at the key words of the sketchy explanation he had managed to pick out. Judy, sensing his panic, came to Vince's rescue.

"Don't worry, Mr Fairchild. This isn't America with your rattlesnakes and bears and what-not. There's nothing on that mountain much bigger or dangerous than a chaffinch. Anyway, you'll be able to ride up there and rescue her, like one of those heroic Mexican chaps you were telling us all about last night."

A boyish grin spread across Fairchild's face.

"I'll saddle up Minotaur for you. He's the biggest horse here and so should be able to carry you both back."

Judy looked cross to where Death-Watch and the others were grazing.

"I see the horses came back, those naughty little blighters. Not the first time they've come home alone. At least they are still saddled up and ready to go."

Judy wandered off to give her wards a superficial dressing down, and Vince provided a few more details about the previous night to Fairchild. This was very much Vince's chance to frame the event in a positive light, so he focused on the parts where he had rushed to help Susan, carried her to a safe bit of rock and then protected them both through the night before heading out into the wilderness to find help. He left out the part about the miraculous recovery of Susan's back as she leapt on top of him.

Judy soon returned to the yard with Minotaur and the other three horses, and then gave them a final public telling off for being naughty for the benefit of Vince and Fairchild. Fairchild then nipped inside to change his shirt to something more heroic and put on his authentic cowboy hat that he'd had flown over when he first realised they needed to go pony trekking. Judy was prepared to forego the legal regulations about hard-hats on this occasion, considering the circumstances, and that Fairchild hadn't paid yet.

***

Up on the mountain, Susan and Emily had bonded.

It seemed there is nothing like a common enemy to bring two warring parties together. History has shown this time and again. Genghis Khan brought together the rival nomadic tribes of North West Asia to create the Mongol army that would wage war against their enemies in Eurasia. Alexander the Great united the squabbling factions of Corinth to then lead Greece in his campaigns against the Persian Empire and Asia Minor. The warring factions of Scotland were united by William Wallace to fight the common enemy of the English. And now, the Ratcliffes and the Fairchilds were united in their distaste for Vincent Crow.

Emily was against Vince because she believed Vince had tried to put some moves on Susan during the night; Susan was against Vince because she had always hated him, and now he was at the centre of her current feelings of embarrassment and anger.

It was just as they had run out of bad things to say against the Midlander, and were discussing how they might go shopping in Regent Street next week, just the two of them, that the cavalry rounded the corner. At the head of the charge was Fairchild. He was towering above his fellow cavalrymen in his Stetson and looking every inch the hero, all the way down to his war wounded, bandaged foot and devastatingly impressive moustache. Behind was Judy on Death-Watch, and leading Green-Tiger behind them was Vince and Cockchafer.

Fairchild beamed at Susan from beneath the brim of his cowboy hat. Susan beamed back at Fairchild as Vince, Judy and Emily all tried to push her onto the top of the horse in front of Fairchild. Minotaur beamed at no one. Had he realised this was the deal, he would have bolted, much has Death-Watch had had the sense to do the previous afternoon. Overall it was the least romantic or elegant vision of a gallant knight rescuing his fair maiden in the history of such events. The wilds of the British Isles has seen its fair share of chivalry and noble gestures over the centuries, so to come bottom in such things is quite an achievement.

Trade-up time

The return journey to London was very similar to the outward one from Vince's perspective. This time the fair weather was in Wales, and it was increasingly miserable as they approached London. The cramped nature of the car had not improved and the women were both still united in their hatred for Vince. Fortunately, Fairchild was still very impressed with him. After all, Vince had protected the girls on the mountain, risked life and limb to fetch help, and enabled Fairchild to return the hero with his woman clinging to him side-saddle on a big horse. Most of all, the 'Zapata-theory' (as he was now calling it) had worked magnificently. The aim had been for Susan and Emily to know each other better. As a result of his effort, it was now as if now they were sisters they were so close. Life in the Fairchild household had got better and better since Vince had arrived on the scene. He would have to show his appreciation.

***

Two weeks later, Fairchild called Vince into his study in his Richmond home. The previous day, his daughter Emily had left for Paris as part of the continuation of her gap year travels. Fairchild was pleased. She was expanding her horizons and seeing new things. It was all a part of her becoming a responsible adult woman. Best of all, Emily now seemed to be getting on much better with Susan, and they had left on good terms. Despite his desire to bring his family closer together, he felt that Emily's departure meant that he could return his life to something resembling normality. He was not used to having his daughter around, and the added complications that Susan had brought to his usual bachelor lifestyle were quite enough for now.

All of this meant that, since their return from Wales, the need for a chauffeur was less evident. Emily had lost all interest in using Vince's driving services, and besides, she was now in Paris. Susan had never seemed to get on very well with Vince, and always preferred to drive herself. Maybe it was because he drove too fast. However, Fairchild couldn't deny that the reason for his current happiness was all down to Vince. All of this Fairchild explained to Vince from behind his writing desk, as Vince sat in the leather chair opposite.

"So you see Vince, Susan and I don't really need a chauffeur any more. I'm grateful for all you've done, so I want to set you up in some other way. Pull a few strings for you. Get you a new job."

At that moment, Susan arrived to fuss over Fairchild with tea and biscuits. She was surprised to find Vince with him.

Her smile dropped as she saw the bain of her life consulting with Fairchild. Vince had to go, far away, and she had to make sure of it.

"I was just talking to Vince about what his future might look like. Maybe one of the neighbours needs a driver, or perhaps one of the set down at the river club?"

Keeping your friends close but your enemies closer didn't work for Susan. She wanted as much distance between herself and Vince as possible.

"What about a job closer to your family up in the Midlands, Vince?"

"I daw no about that, Mrs Ratcliffe. It'd be nice to see me nan again, but I'm not sure people in our area really use chauffeurs a lot. They tend to drive themselves if they've got a car. If not they just take the bus."

"What did you do up there before you started driving then?"

"I was in the hospitality and catering business, Mr Fairchild. My last job in the Midlands was at a public house."

Fairchild smiled as he reminisced about his night in the quaint and rustic Welsh tavern. His eyes glazed over at the thought of all the fascinated locals looking on at the exotic American dispensing invaluable knowledge and holding their unwavering attention.

"We should buy a tavern, Susan! Somewhere up north where Vince comes from, full of English charm and warm beer. Vince can run it for us. You used to be in the hotel trade Suzie, perhaps you can help him set it up."

Susan nodded.

"Vince and I can go to the kitchen and discuss the details."

She headed for the door and beckoned to Vince to follow. Vince failed to sense the air of menace that accompanied the gesture.

Once they were out of Fairchild's earshot, Susan turned to Vince with a face like thunder.

"I don't know how you're doing this. But you need to get as far away from our lives as possible!"

"Mrs Ratcliffe? Mr Fairchild asked me to talk to him. This is his idea not mine."

"Very well, Vincent. Then this is my idea. You go back to the grim suburb of the Black Country that you crawled out from. Tomorrow at the latest. Today is better. Find a small free-hold pub that's for sale, send me the details and I'll arrange with Jonathan to buy it. You don't talk to Jonathan, you talk to me. After that, all day to day issues you handle yourself. Big issues, say, I don't know, burning down the whole building, for which you already have an impressive record, you call me. Not Jonathan. You don't come back to London. You do not disturb this family."

Vince agreed.

Chapter 6 – Landlord

Delivery

"Vince! There's some bloke at the door with a package. Wants me to sign his pissin' clipboard, but he says he's got nought to do with reading the meter. That Gavin usually comes to read the meter, and he's got one of those new plasticated cards with his photo on it. Mrs Garret let one of these types in once. When she was in the kitchen making tea they took the rent-money right out of her purse and pissin'-well legged it before the kettle was even boiled! Of course Mrs Garret's circulation has been playing her up lately and she's had to start wearing one of them elasticated socks to stop all her blood sinking all the way down to her pissin' feet."

Vince was already reaching the bottom of the stairs by the time his nan had completed her opening monologue and diagnosis of Mrs Garret's blood circulation. His nan was a quiet soul in the winter months. She was content to sit in the kitchen with a brew of stewed tea, a portable TV regurgitating tedious daytime chatter, and an extra bar on the electric fire when she was feeling extravagant. However, that was during what Vince regarded as her 'hibernation mode'. Much as the scaly alligator basks on the banks of the everglade swamps in the morning sun to energise its body, attune its senses, and prepare for the day's hunt, so too did his nan develop an unnecessary enthusiasm for participating in society during the warmer months.

"It's alright Nan. I'll sort this."

Vince had reached the door and positioned himself between the courier and his nan to protect the former from further tales of the benign challenges of Mrs Garret. Having signed for the package, he returned to his room to review the contents.

***

It was the end of August when Susan's lawyers finished checking the documents, gave them their professional approval, and returned them to her. They had been deemed legally acceptable and so she brought them to Fairchild in his study for his signature. Once he had scrawled his inky mark across the bottom he became the proud owner of The Carrot and Jam Kettle, a local pub with local charm. He then signed a second document, a contract which declared Vince as manager of said public house, and with free-rein to run the establishment as he saw fit. Susan had photocopied both and then gave the original employment contract and a copy of the ownership documents to a courier to deliver to the heart of the Midlands.

Vince felt that trade-up number five held a lot of promise. Previous jobs in the last year had fallen into a category that Vince's mind had classified as 'menial'. Always a servant to the masters of the industry, never the master. Only at the Armstrong Hotel had he been in the brief position of supervising others, and this was a temporary thing that would have been taken away again by Masterton, had the hotel not been destroyed before he'd returned. This time it was different. He was the manager of a pub. Manager meant that you managed people, and therefore inherently implied that you were no longer at the very bottom of the heap. This had been the kind of genuine trade-up Vince had been thinking of when he'd planned his prison break from the high security confines of the washing-up sink at the end of the previous year. Finally he was on his way. Three months of pub management, and then who knew? By then he might have good contacts in the breweries and get a better job there managing more people. He would be like Mr Fairchild and move in the social circles that required him to join golf clubs and attending posh dinners where there were important speakers. That was where you made contacts and developed money making schemes. It was clear that, up until now, Vince's trading life had simply been bouncing around within the same menial category. Now he had stepped up to a whole new level and would have to make the most of the opportunity. There was no looking back, Vincent Crow was about to hit the big time.

The pub

It had been almost eight months since Vince had first escaped from the indistinct and sleepy Midland suburbs to adventure in the big city smoke of the capital. However, a surprising amount had happened in his absence. Notably, The Carrot and Jam Kettle had been put on the market. This was fortuitous indeed as he was due to identify a pub for Fairchild to purchase, and for himself to manage. Indeed, it was on the same evening that he had returned to the Midlands that his nan had given him the news that the "pissin' Carrot" was up for sale, would probably get turned into one of them "pissin' wine-bars, and encourage the wrong crowd" before launching into various scenarios of how the wrong crowd would negatively influence her daily routine.

Vince had taken a few moments to sum up in his mind the pros and cons of becoming manager of his former workplace. In its favour, he was familiar with the way that the pub was run, familiar with the clientele, and it was close enough for him to keep an eye on his nan. On the downside, he wasn't sure why it was for sale, and it was possible that the wife of the previous owner was eight months pregnant with Vince's child. However, he hadn't yet worked out how to identify any other freehold pubs that were on the market or how to negotiate their purchase. Also, he was very much overdue for a trade-up, so there was little choice but to go for it.

To the eternal relief of Natalie Sedgwick, by February she found that she had not fallen pregnant to anyone. This meant that whatever had happened between her and Vince had not resulted in an unwanted child. Any future sprogs, had they turned up, would definitely have been sired by her husband. In contrast, the absence of a developing foetus had left Dennis Sedgwick desperately disappointed with life. He had set his heart on fatherhood. Unfortunately, he had assumed that once the decision had been made to have a baby, an egg would be fertilized almost immediately and his progeny would be on its way. After all, a man doesn't go to the extremes of investing in a small selection of fluffy toys and baby clothes only to discover a month later that there are no off-spring on the immediate horizon to receive them. Taking into account the huge efforts people go to to protect themselves against becoming pregnant, it is not unreasonable to assume that once you stop with the condoms, the pill, and being too drunk to function, then pregnancy would arrive with a certain degree of immediacy.

He was not a patient man and had even been known to leave a football match at half time if his team was a couple of goals down, rather than wait and give them a chance to catch up in the second half. His impatience and frustration on the baby issue was severely compounded by Natalie's evident lack of personal devastation at the revelation that she was not instantly up the duff. Mrs Sedgwick senior, the battle-axe that was Dennis's mother, took great pleasure in pointing this out numerous times to her despondent son.

By March, Dennis had left Natalie once again, and had moved back in with his mother. The permanency of the move was compounded when he took a bar-manager job in the neighbouring town. The stars had aligned for 'the battle-axe' to start weaving her intricate and interfering webs to ensure a better future for both her son and herself. This started at the Gardening Club day-out to the Chelsea Flower Show. She had convinced Dennis to accompany her on the day out, and then craftily set about teaming him up with Angela-Rose Harrison. She was a mid-thirties, sensible girl, unattached, and with a limited sense of humour and even more limited conversation. She was not unrefined and common like Natalie, but had an attractive, petite figure and dressed in a very presentable way. She was polite to the degree that she would listen and show interest in Dennis even when he was going on about football. She was also dull enough to be delighted that someone was interested enough to keep talking to her. However, Angela-Rose Harrison was not some randomly chosen daughter of one of the battle-axe's many Gardening Club cronies, who had also been conned into the day out on the pretence that chaperons were required to stop aging members of the group wandering off and getting lost. This astutely contrived pairing was a sly and tactical move, on a great many levels.

Firstly, of course was the need to permanently separate Dennis from that awful woman he'd married, and replace her quickly with one of the class that was presentable in Mrs Sedgwick's circle of polite society. Secondly, Mrs Sedgwick was both ambitious and devious. The seat of power at the Gardening Club lay with the panel members of the judging committee. It was a cut-throat business, and Mrs Beatrix Harrison, mother of Angela-Rose, was the long-standing 'kingmaker' of the Gardening Club committee. Years of toadying and turning up to fund-raising events with a home-made sponge cake simply got one to the extreme edges of the inner circle. To progress along the leafy pergola of power demanded tactics far beyond those of proven home-baking skills. A pact was needed that went deeper. Mrs Sedgwick's scheme to unite Dennis and Angela-Rose would bring together the two houses of the Harrisons and the Sedgwicks. Once a child was conceived, the two families would be bonded for eternity with a shared blood-line. From thenceforth, the right of Mrs Sedgwick to judge the colour and shape of the Alicante tomatoes at the summer fete vegetable competition would never be challenged. Her power would be absolute, and the dream was within her grasp.

Unlike Natalie, Angela-Rose had proven to be an instant baby-making machine and soon fell pregnant with Dennis's child. Beatrix Harrison, apparently unaware of the extent to Mrs Sedgwick's meddling, immediately colluded with Mrs Sedgwick to plan a summer wedding before Angela-Rose began to show too much. Together they found a good lawyer to ensure Dennis got a quick divorce from Natalie. Dennis Sedgwick was delighted with his new life. Within a few months of walking away from Natalie he had a good job and a devoted and attentive wife. More than that, there was a baby on the way that would be forced to enjoy football and support Wolverhampton Wanderers whether he wanted to or not. The option of a little girl arriving had never crossed his mind.

All of this had meant that The Carrot and Jam Kettle had been on the market for about a month or so. Once the wedding was done, Dennis planned to make a new start at running a Bed and Breakfast in North Devon that he and Angela-Rose would manage together. The plan was to find one with a nice large garden, which would then become a sort of weekend retreat for Gardening Club members. This was not only good for trade but would also entice his new mother-in-law to play her part as a key benefactor, and act as a guarantor against the mortgage they would need. The only down side of this was the increased length of the journey to the Molineux Stadium for him and Junior to yell encouragement from the side lines at Wolverhampton Wanderers.

Since his departure from The Carrot and Jam Kettle, Dennis had allowed Natalie to run the business and take a salary. This was a far easier option than having to deal with Natalie, as she did have a bit of a temper on her, and Dennis was not good at confrontations. However, the lawyers had finalised the divorce and helped get the pub on the market. Now that it was up for sale, Natalie's immediate future was in the hands of whoever took it over.

Return to 'The Carrot'

Over recent months, Natalie had started to look like she'd fallen over in a curtain shop, and failed to brush herself down properly once she'd got up. Where once there was bling, there were now tassels and ethnic dangly things. She had been rejected as both a wife and a future mother at the same time, and her depression had manifested itself in a vision of un-shapely floral shades of brown. Clearly this was not good for business, as the old men who frequented the bar didn't want to focus their blurry beer-goggles on upholstery, but needed to be spared the effort of imagination when thinking about what might lie beneath. Natalie's previous wardrobe selection had been much more accommodating in this regard.

The full reasons for her despondency were three-fold.

Firstly, she had lost Dennis. Even she was surprised that this had hit her so hard, as he was not the greatest catch. However, there's no predicting how emotions are going to affect you.

Secondly, there was her mild disappointment of not having a baby, as when one didn't arrive after all the initial hype, she decided that she would have quite liked one. Other people her age already had some. Whilst tantrums and nappy changes did not particularly appeal, not joining in with motherhood excluded you from various conversations and mothers-clubs, along with the opportunity to blame any really obscure opinion on the fact you were a mother. This also seemed to prevent anyone being allowed to argue against any bouts of insane opinion you imposed.

Thirdly, there was the overall state of her current prospects. When Dennis had bought the pub it had not come cheap and had required a very large overdraft. Nearly all of the money they made was ploughed back into the bank to pay off the interest on the loan and keep the bailiffs from the door. However, since Dennis had left The Carrot and Jam Kettle, trade had fallen off as well. Surprisingly it appeared that a number of locals frequented the place 'because' and not 'in spite' of Dennis droning on about football. All this meant that if Dennis had not managed to sell the pub when he did, and give all proceedings to the bank, they would have had to file for bankruptcy anyway. In a divorce settlement, half of nothing is still nothing, and when your husband hired a better lawyer than you did, sometimes it's even less than that. Therefore, her only hope was to convince the new owners of the pub to let her continue to work there. Otherwise she would be out on the streets.

It was early on an overcast Monday evening when Vince wandered into her pub for the first time since January. Natalie had her back to the doors, organising the till in preparation for the evening shift.

"Alright, Nat?"

Vince wandered up to the bar and sat at a bar-stool. It was six in the evening. Opening time was 6.30pm but he knew that ordinarily the door would be unlocked a little beforehand to let in any staff that were on that night. Natalie looked round from where she had been emptying some small plastic bags of change into the till.

"Vince! What brings you back? Didn't we agree you were never to return if I wrote that bloomin' reference for you?"

Vince nodded thoughtfully. He'd forgotten about that, and subsequently it hadn't made it on to the cons list when deciding to choose a pub.

"Well, it doesn't matter anyway, Vince. Dennis is gone. Left me for some country-club slut his mother lined him up with. Bastard."

Vince tried to take in the new information, whilst attempting to concentrate over the jangling noise of the various decorative attachments to Natalie's clothes.

"I see, Nat. So why then are you still here?"

"Dennis sold up. I say sold up – gave the place back to the bank more like. I was phoned up by the new owner, some American bloke. He asked me to spend a week doing a handover to his new manager, when he arrives. He says the manager will pay me when he gets here, so I might as well. I could be out on the streets after that, so better to get some cash in hand."

Vince cleared his throat. He'd never been good at explaining complicated things, and what he was about to say seemed to require a good clear explanation.

"I'm the new manager, Nat."

"Of what?"

"The Carrot and Jam Kettle. I'm the new manager. That was Mr Fairchild you were on the phone with. I was working for him down in London, and helped him out with his family on a pony-trek so he said he'd buy me a pub to manage. Perhaps, you could start the handover by giving me the keys, Nat. I'm thinking that I'll move in to the flat above the pub."

Natalie gazed at Vince with a stunned look, all facial muscles locked in position. Had she been wearing her usual mud-pack of foundation it would have been in no danger of cracking. Eventually, she ventured a question:

"When do you think you'll move in?"

"Well Nat, me nan's planning to do a shepherd's pie with gravy on Wednesday, so we're probably looking at the night after that."

Thursday night

Vince arrived at the pub, and crossed the threshold carrying a couple of large plastic bags with his clothes in them. He let himself in with his own key and headed up the stairs to the flat above the bar.

"Alright Nat – you in?"

"Evening Vince, I've just put the kettle on – you want a cuppa?"

It had been three days since Vince announced his intention to move in to the flat above the pub. Since that time, Vince and Natalie had spent a lot of time talking through their current situations. Considering their vastly different pasts, there were a number of similarities:

Natalie had recently lost her husband, Dennis, to a woman whose lineage in gardening club circles was deemed impressive, and was also carrying Dennis's unborn child. Subsequently, Natalie was currently very insecure in her social interactions. Her financial future had also been very insecure as there was no guarantee of work after she handed over the pub.

Vince, meanwhile, had recently been separated from Emily, and despite this had always been completely socially inept anyway. In addition, he was particularly insecure in his working life, having never run a pub before. The combination of these two sets of inadequacies was either going to lead to a disastrous outcome, or a great opportunity for a new beginning. Together they had decided to aim for the latter.

The deal was simple. Firstly, Vince would run the bar, and Natalie would run the kitchens. Secondly, Natalie would teach Vince how to run the bar and also how to manage the pub in terms of finance, ordering, stock taking, and tax returns; also Vince would let Natalie share the upstairs flat, rent free. Finally, should either one of them suggest that they lock the doors of the pub and try to drink all of the optics on the back of the bar, the other had to refuse and send the suggestee to bed with a sympathetic cup of cocoa.

Over the next few weeks the new partnership developed and started to work well. Natalie slowly came out of her depression and stopped dressing like a batik Indian bedspread with tassels, and Vince became fairly competent at bar tending.

In his previous brief encounter with the bar-hogging punters of The Carrot and Jam Kettle, Vince had astutely worked out that a number of punters rolled in specifically so that they could be bored senseless by Dennis pontificating about football. As a substitute to this tedium, Vince had ordered a large TV to hang-up at one end of the bar, and a smaller one for behind the bar.

Footy on satellite TV more than compensated for the lack of Dennis, and actually enticed a few more customers in. It was also great for Vince, as by and large it rescued him from having to talk to people. Vince didn't mind football, although he didn't follow it with a passion. However, many of his football punters were there to escape their families and troubles for the evening, and the resultant football talk was actually a euphemistic counselling session. A punter in this category may have the words 'It's so depressing to see our star player being poached by one of the richer clubs in the premiership' coming out of their mouths. Meanwhile, they were actually thinking 'I'm worried my wife is going to leave me for the wealthy bloke who works as a manager at B&Q, as he's always hanging around her till and chatting her up'. If Vince didn't catch on to this double meaning, and said something non-committal like, 'It'd be good for that bloke's career though wouldn't it?' the conversation could get very emotional quite quickly.

The conversation challenge for Vince was worse mid-week as, in the absence of fresh football results, conversation-less customers would either sit at the bar and expect Vince to provide topics for conversation, or else they would regurgitate exact copies of conversations they'd all had on a previous occasion, sometimes only a few days before. Satellite TV was therefore an act of genius on Vince's part, and appreciated by both customer and bartender alike.

Natalie was also revitalised. In the absence of Dennis, she had spent a lot of afternoons in recent months watching day-time TV with a large glass of gin for company. Through this experience, she had learned many things. This included the notion that no matter how many colourful people with rural accents you add to the mix, gardening will always be inherently dull. She also learned that when chat shows run out of topics or their special guests cancel they do make-over specials to embarrass ordinary people.

She also began to learn that a large glass of gin in the afternoon didn't make her the most pleasant company when she got behind the bar for the evening shift. However, despite these many challenges, she had also sat through a lot of cookery programmes. Through this process she was enlightened to the concept that food wasn't about just sticking a frozen pie in a microwave and deep-frying some chips. Of course, Dennis had greatly influenced the content of The Carrot and Jam Kettle's menu, and had aimed to provide a similar fare to the type of greasy edibles you would find at a football match or kebab shop. Natalie decided this new beginning would see the start of a new menu. The traditional deep-fried favourites remained for the long-term retainers. However, a specials board was introduced and a number of homemade specialities were developed for the more discerning clientele. A lounge area was set up to enable people to enjoy their food away from the football TV, and gradually trade picked up. Natalie's new lease of life was only, in part, due to her new cookery hobby. Having Vince around had made a difference, too. He was quiet, kind, not obsessed with football, and not at the beck and call of the evil dragon that had brought him into this world. She was starting to see what a happy life without Dennis could be like.

Innovation

Vince dried up the final pint glass and placed it on the shelf above the bar with the others. It had been yet another quiet mid-week evening. October had arrived and with it the dull overcast weather that delivered news of the impending winter that lay ahead. He looked out of the dormer window at the end of the lounge and studied the orange light in the pub car park, which was engulfed in a drizzly haze. The nights were starting to draw in and the suburban pub-goers were choosing to spend their week-nights in front of the TV soap operas, rather than venture through the drizzle to reach the pub. The clientele was largely reduced to the die-hard beer swillers and those escapees who considered that a pint of best offered more support and comfort to their lives than their family ever could.

Natalie wandered round to the front of the bar, put two plates of Beef Peposo with couscous on the bar towels in front of where Vince was standing. From her apron pocket she produced some cutlery and placed it between the plates and the beer pump for the local bitter. Vince reciprocated the gesture by pouring Natalie a glass of wine, and himself a pint of lager.

"Quiet tonight again, Nat."

Vince moved to the other side of the bar and joined her for the uneaten special of the day.

"It's the season, Vince. People don't want to venture out in the cold. Besides, the months before and after Christmas are the quiet ones. They're either saving their money for the parties and presents, or are paying off the credit cards afterwards."

"Maybe we need something extra to bring the people in. Maybe a darts night, or a pool night at the beginning of the week?"

As he said it, Vince thought back to the pool night he had attended at The Crown with Roy Buckworth and his cronies. Since that time he had clearly tried to stitch up his co-workers at the factory with his out-sourcing scheme, and then walked out of there with Kaleena without letting anyone know. Did he really want to join a pub pool league where it was probable those very same people would eventually have to come into his pub and compete?

"I know that this is your pub now, Vince, but I don't really want this to become a sports bar more than it has to. Besides, having a pub team can be more effort than it's worth. People are enthusiastic to start with and then you join the league. After that some of them start dropping out and you can't get enough people together for the away matches. It's really not worth the hassle."

Vince was quite relieved to hear that Natalie was unenthusiastic about his idea, albeit for different reasons than his.

"A pub quiz then, Nat?"

"Tried it before, Vince. Dennis did the questions for a sports quiz, and if you didn't know every bloomin' obscure detail about Wolverhampton Wanderers then it was impossible to join in. A bit like one of his conversations really."

"What about a live band?"

Natalie did not react immediately with a put-down for the idea. Instead she considered it carefully. More dull sports nonsense like her dull ex-husband was likely to send her back to batik and chime-bell induced depression. Some live music, however, might put a bit of life and party back into the place.

"What did you have in mind, Vince?"

Band night

'Trumpet-Cup and the Spoon-billed Coots, with front man Terry Stubbles. One night only. Wednesday 15th October'.

Vince stood back and admired the notice he had made for the front window. Only a few weeks ago he had become manager of his first pub, and now he was hosting his first ever live booking. The idea had come to him a week or so earlier. Subsequently, and also in an attempt to distract a couple of bar-proppers from engaging him in a debate about some footballing rule to do with kicking the ball to the side when there was an injury, he had told them about his band idea. It seemed the bar-proppers knew a few people in the music game, and two days later, in strolled Terry Stubbles.

Terry had leaned across the bar, ordered a pint of lager and then began his sales pitch. This started with a very elaborate explanation of how 'Stubbles' was his real name, which was much less usual than 'Stubble', and in fact his ancestry went back to the Stoke-On-Trent Stubbles. Vince's awareness of his own ancestry was limited to the existence of his nan, so this didn't particularly draw him in to the degree that Terry had hoped for.

The remaining sales pitch extended to a slightly crumpled gas bill that had a song list scrawled on the back, an explanation of the band members' individual talents, and a presentation of Terry's three most relevant tattoos. This included a V-shaped guitar on his left arm, a skull on his left shoulder, and the phrase 'March or Die' written on his back in letters that dripped blood. (At the time of tattooing, Terry had known this only as a Motorhead song, and not realised that declaring this in print on his body would somewhat imply that he had joined the French Foreign Legion in his recent past. This ignorance was still the case today, as very few people he showed it to also made the connection, and those that did had thought better than to explain it.)

It was an unusual interview but Terry put forward a clear and convincing case. Also, Vince was concerned that there was a certain wildness to Terry that suggested if he didn't get the gig then unwelcome repercussions were a possibility.

The gig was subsequently booked. The back end of the lounge would be rearranged so that the drums and amps could be set up next to the fish tank. Trumpet-cup and the Spoon-billed Coots would arrive on the Saturday afternoon for a sound check, and agreed they would make sure the fish were plugged back in afterwards to re-oxygneate the tank before the band needed the plug again in the evening.

Even Vince's nan had decided she'd come along and chew on half a mild to see what all the fuss was about.

Terry Stubbles

It was, in fact, Terry Stubbles' first headlining gig with the Spoon-bills. His previous band, 'The Charcoals', had split the year before. Terry had done a couple of months inside for GBH, and on return found that the band members, in his absence, had all moved on artistically. In fact, Kev on bass, following the surgery to remove glass from his forehead, had moved on physically as well, in an attempt to avoid being a recurring victim of GBH. Since then Terry had been putting together a new line-up.

A feature of the time with live music in the Midlands was that the bands all tended to idolise their local heroes. Renowned members of their musical heritage extended to Ozzy Ozborne, Judas Priest, Slade and Led Zeppelin. Subsequently, all guitar bands wanted to try to sound like Led Zeppelin or do covers of their songs. Finding a line-up that was prepared to go for more contemporary music, that non-aging rockers wanted to listen to in local venues, was a challenge. However, despite this stipulation, the Spoon-bills had acquired a drummer called Des, and then in recent months gained some momentum and taken in Lippy on acoustic and Gail on base. The final member of the band was Terry's current girlfriend, Lil. She had learned trumpet for a while at school and, with Terry's support, had re-learned a few trumpet-based classics. Many of these were Van Morrison related, as contemporary music is generally quite limited in the trumpet department.

The Spoon-bills' set included some songs that Terry himself had penned, along with a bunch of covers. The rule was that all covers had to come from the last five years, to maximise the number of people in the audience who might have heard of them (with an amending clause, such that this rule didn't extend to trumpet-based songs). The five-year rule was based on the observations Terry had made when performing with The Charcoals. It was noticeable that when performing a cover from the seventies it was only really his Uncle Keith, propping up the bar at the back of the venue with a cigarette and half a stout, who knew any of the words. He had stewed over his observation of this phenomenon whilst in prison, and had come up with the five-year rule as a result. Had it not been for him then drunkenly hooking up with Lil on his first Friday night after release, that resulted in the trumpet-based amendment, it could have been quite a good idea.

A few practice sessions and they were ready to hit the bottom of the ladder, which might help them to eventually reach the big time should they display some genuine talent and not fall out with each other in the process. The first rung of this remarkably long ladder was to be The Carrot and Jam Kettle gig.

The gig

Bandnight had started well. The pub was fairly full. Vince had also nailed a few flyers to telegraph poles in the neighbourhood as a key marketing strategy. A few more locals than usual turned up to see what was happening. Also, about ten people who were mates with the band members arrived early and started drinking, which was good for business, and had basically covered Terry Stubbles' fee before he even started playing. In fact, Terry had started drinking quite heavily around the same time, so had pretty much offset his earnings before he started the actual gig. In his own mind, however, this was just part of 'rock and roll'. He explained to Vince that going on stage with a few drinks for courage helped him deliver his vibrant on-stage persona. Vince was concerned that it would also deliver a slurring lyric-forgetting performance, but chose not to point this out.

Since the forthcoming performance of the legendary 'Terry Stubbles' had been displayed on the board at the front of the pub, a number of the clientele had furnished Vince with tales of his infamy. These included the time Terry was busted for dealing drugs, the time Terry was busted for handling stolen goods, and also the time that Stubbles had drunkenly, but purposely, crashed his Ford Escort into the front window of the new Balti on the high street, when he believed his then girlfriend was having an affair with the owner. In fact, she was merely within the Balti restaurant and chatting to the owner as part of the acceptable process in which to order a Balti – a situation which Stubbles, in his temperamental state of alcohol blurred confusion, had significantly misread. Surprisingly, the story of being jailed for GBH had yet to be told at the bar of The Carrot and Jam Kettle. However, the existing information was enough to let Vince know that Stubbles was to be humoured to avoid any unnecessary dramatics.

By 8.30pm the band had started their first set. Trumpet-Cup and the Spoon-billed Coots were quite good, considering it was their first gig. The injection to the bar of a bit of a party atmosphere was appreciated by all but the most hardened football fans that refused to be distracted from their sporting interests. Lil's visual qualities were more attractive than her trumpeting ones and so the male members of the audience were able to employ there well-practiced genetic advantage of tuning out that part out of their hearing, and just focused on what she looked like.

The first set was about fifty minutes, and then Terry Stubbles promised they would be back after a twenty minute break and a pint. He returned his guitar to its stand with a deafening wail of feedback from the speakers, and then sauntered up to the bar for a free jar of Guinness, which was part of the fee as agreed by Vince.

Lil and Des

It was after Terry Stubbles had drained his second mid-gig pint of Guinness that he decided a trip to the toilets was increasingly in order. Having announced loudly to those around him that he was 'goin' for a piss', he removed himself from his bar-stool and headed round the corner of the bar towards the corridor, past the stairs where the gents were. As he passed through the crowded bar area, he caught sight of his girlfriend, Lil, who was in the far corner of the room. His vision also settled on Des the drummer, who had his arm around her and had just kissed her on the neck.

Rage erupted in Stubbles with the fury of a man who has a reputation of uncontrolled violence. He yelled out with the volume and drama of a distressed camel that had decided it had been ridden quite enough for one day and wasn't going to go along with the whole 'beast of burden' thing any more until it got a decent rest and a food bag. In a swift and violent reaction, he swung his arm over the end of the bar, smashing five or more glasses of drinks, which shattered against the back of the bar. Silence engulfed the whole pub. Des and Lil stared back in horror at the manically wild eyes of Terry Stubbles, whose anger was visibly boiling over.

It was at this very moment that Natalie emerged from the kitchens at the door to the side of the bar with a tray of meals. This included sausage and chips for Trevor, who had been downing beer since lunch time, and needed to soak up some of the alcohol if his planned forthcoming stagger was going to be sufficient to propel him all the way to his house two streets over. There was also a medium rump steak for Lippy on acoustic, whose energy was so drained by the first performance of the evening that he needed renewed verve and mushroom sauce if he was to carry on. Terry's reaction to Natalie appearing at his side was to smash the tray of food from her hands, letting it crash to the floor at her feet. He immediately grabbed the steak knife from the floor and held it to Natalie's throat, warm steak juices slowly running down the handle and dripping onto Natalie's shoulder.

"Don't yaw lot move, or I'll cut her!"

"Vince!"

Natalie cried out as Terry started to drag her past the entrance of the kitchen and then up the stairs that led to the apartment above the pub.

Vince, who had been at the end of the bar pouring a beer for a customer, was aware that Terry, by his own admittance, was off for a slash, as he had loudly announced that this was the case. Vince was particularly confused by the fact that on reaching the end of the bar Terry had then smashed up the place and then kidnapped his flat-mate/ co-manager at knifepoint. Vince rushed past the end of the bar and to the bottom of the stairs to see the raging Terry and his struggling kidnappee round the top of the landing and into the upstairs flat.

"Nan – call the police! I'll go up and talk to him."

Vince's nan had been sitting at the bar with Trevor, discussing the need for a new pelican crossing in the middle of her street to save the effort of traipsing all of the way down to the traffic lights at the end of the road. She downed her glass of wine before heading round to the other side of the bar where the phone was, and dialled 999. Vince, meanwhile, headed up the stairs with the enthusiasm of one who had not yet grasped the seriousness of the situation.

Vince's nan had slowly pressed the telephone buttons with the apprehension of one whose house was still fitted with a big beige telephone that had a circular dial in the middle of it, and began to address the polite lady who had inquired which service was being required:

"Yam right there. Is that the pigs? The woman that used to be married to the last landlord's been taken up the pissin' stairs by the singer of the band with a steak knife. Trevor ordered sausage and chips and now that's on the pissin' floor as well. There's pissin' glass everywhere back here – you should see the state of it. These youths couldn't behave like that in my day you know. Respect for your pissin' elders, or you got the belt. My old man didn't stand for it, and people knew their place. Course, after a twelve-hour shift down the mines you expected to come home with yaw pissin' dinner on the table and god help you if it wasn't. Some lads chucked a bin full of rubbish over Mrs Garret's front wall the other day, and the council said there was nothing they could do due to the cutbacks and she'd have to clean it up herself. The government should lock-up the pissin' lot of them."

The lady on the switchboard was about to asked where the person was calling from, and if perhaps there was someone else she could talk to. However, Vince's nan had already put the receiver down, feeling that sufficient information had been imparted to allow the authorities to get on with the job in hand. Having turned around and realised that she was now behind the bar and that Vince had gone, Vince's nan's practical instincts kicked in. She decided to cover for her absent grandson, and so started to pull a pint for one of the customers.

Negotiation

Vince arrived at the top of the stairs with slightly less enthusiasm than the adrenalin had given him when he left from the bottom of the stairs. The door to the flat had remained ajar, and he slowly pushed it open, calling out as he did so.

"Yaw alright Terry. You seemed a bit upset like, back there? I'd thought you were going for a piss?"

Natalie was sitting on one of the stools that were part of the breakfast bar in the corner of the room. Her pleading eyes stared at Vince in desperation as her tears washed the eye shadow and mascara from her face. In fact, she was crying so much it was now running down her neck and mixing with the steak juice that was deposited there earlier. Terry stood behind her, knife still at her throat.

"Don't come no closer Vince, I meant what I said!"

"But why Terry? I don't understand."

"Des, that pathetic excuse for a drummer was getting off with my missus when me back was turned, wasn't he. I never trusted him. Only let him join the band cos he's a mate of me brother's. I should have never trusted her either. Bitch."

"Sorry Terry. I had no idea. Is there anything I can do to help?"

"Unless you can have this piss for me Vincent, probably not."

Vince did recall that Terry's need to ease himself had been why he had left his spot at the bar in the first place, and this added frustration had probably contributed to the current series of events. He studied the situation carefully. It was a bit like the mind-puzzle at school with the farmer getting the fox, chicken and grain across the river but only two at a time. Vince had never got past the logic of why you would have need to own both a fox and a chicken in the first place, and therefore why the answer wasn't to simply let the fox return to its natural habitat and let the farmer get on with his chicken raising. The side of the river that this needed to take place on was then largely irrelevant. In this seemingly parallel case, the frustrated farmer was Terry, with Natalie and a steak-knife as his cargo, who somehow had to cross the obstacle of a bathroom-stop without incident. Terry was not going to release Nat so he could go to the bathroom; he was not going to take Nat with him and then put down the knife. From Vince's perspective and acute ability for lateral thinking, the only solution was if the bathroom came to Terry. Vince glanced up at the large vase on the bookcase. This was the very same one that had replaced the vase of chrysanthemums broken by Vince after his first night in the flat, back in January.

"I'll get you down that vase and empty it. You can take a leak in that if you like."

Terry nodded. Vince stood on an armchair to reach the vase at the top of the bookshelf. He removed some dried flowers that Natalie had displayed in it, and put it on the stool next to Terry before returning to the area near the bookcase and turning his back.

The logistics of what happened next remains a secret part of the history of the night's events, known only to the three of them, never to be disclosed. However, the outcome was that within a couple of minutes, Terry was much less uncomfortable and far more open for negotiation.

"So why are you up here with Nat, then Terry, if Des and Lil are the ones you're upset with?"

"I dunno, Vince. I saw Des and Lil, got all angry, and reacted like. They were across the other end of the pub, so I just did this."

As he talked, Terry lowered the knife a little, much to Natalie's relief. A long silence then followed. Natalie was still too petrified to speak, and Vince didn't really know what else to say. It would be unwise to start criticizing Lil and Des as it could make matters worse again. Also, if Terry and Lil got passed Lil's slight indiscretion, Vince would be the one that had said bad things about her. This could then lead to future problems involving hostages and cutlery. After a couple of minutes Terry failed to say anything either, so Vince tried a different tack.

"What if me and Nat go and talk to Lil for you? Maybe get her to come up here and you can both sort things out."

"I don't think there's much to sort out, Vince. That cheating bitch and me is over, and Des has got it coming to him an-all. It's ruined the band. We'll be without a drummer."

Terry put down the knife on the breakfast bar.

"Let Nat come over by me. We can see how to sort this all out then, Terry."

Terry nodded, and the still-sobbing Natalie immediately rushed over to Vince and threw her arms around him, burying her damp and dishevelled face in his chest.

"Now then Terry, there's not really much harm done is there? Just a few broken glasses and plates. A normal Saturday night in a busy pub really. Let's go back down to the bar and you and Lil can talk about it."

Terry agreed, left the knife where it was, and led the way back to the stairs. Natalie was still clinging, limpet-like to Vince, and they descended back down towards the bar.

The bottom of the stairs was, once again, a scene of unexpected events.

Firstly, as Terry placed his foot on the last step of the staircase, there was a large siren wail from the police car that had just arrived outside, in spite of Vince's nan's unhelpful call. This was the distraction which caused Terry to reactively swing to his right, and meant that he failed to spot the trumpet that was swinging violently towards him at high speed from his left. This was on the end of Lil's muscular forearm from where she had been lying in wait for him by the wall at the bottom of the stairs. It connected cleanly with the forehead of Terry, and sent him into an unconscious dive to the floor, landing in the debris of sausage and chips which was still waiting to be cleared up. At this point, two disgruntled police officers marched in to the bar, primarily to address a complaint from their switch board operator about a hoax caller. They found themselves faced with an unconscious man sprawled across the floor, whose face was resting in a rump steak, and bleeding profusely from his forehead. Standing over him like a lion defending its kill, was a wildly aggressive looking woman, brandishing a trumpet spattered with blood. Also of note was a rather elderly woman behind the bar energetically serving drinks, apparently lining up a wide range of colourful cocktails along the length of bar for anyone who had the courage to take them on. The first officer made the astute decision to call for back up, which he decided should include an ambulance.

After about twenty minutes, Vince watched the various emergency services staff leave though the front door with their appropriate charges. He turned to address the new bar-keeping system which had suddenly developed.

"Nan. What yaw doin' behind the bar?"

"Doing your job for you, Vincent. I was pulling pints in public houses while you were still in your pissin' nappies my boy."

Vince's nan turned to the customer in front of her.

"Now love, you wanted a Margarita. Vince! What are you charging for a Margarita in this pissin' bar of yours?"

Vince decided that now was not the time to be concerned with Margaritas. Besides, he still had a weepy Natalie clinging on to him.

"I haven't got time for that now, Nan. I've got a vase filled to the brim with Terry's piss upstairs. I've got to go and sort it out or else the curtains will be reeking with the stench for weeks."

Halloween Cocktail Night

A number of interesting discoveries were made on band night. One of these was that Vince's nan had once worked in a cocktail bar in Torquay – unlikely though that might seem. The Hollywood image of a cocktail bar waitress is a polite attractive young lady, keen to welcome you sweetly to the bar and help you squander your money on extravagant and colourful alcohol. Vince's nan meanwhile, was an aging cardigan-clad pensioner, with an approach to communication that was peppered with colourful, albeit repetitive, language, and who rarely retained a chain of thought beyond the first two or three words of a sentence. Making the link between these two ends of the cocktail waitress spectrum was difficult. However, Vince's nan did seem to know how to mix most of the different drinks, which was more than anyone else who laid a tentative claim to the right to work behind the bar at The Carrot and Jam Kettle.

Another discovery from band night was that becoming a pub with notoriety, in this case being notable for a failed hostage taking situation by a drunken guitarist who was brought down by a tattooed blonde with a trumpet, is very good for business. In fact, since the advantages of notoriety became apparent, Vince arranged for Natalie to do more shifts behind the bar. The customers enjoyed, indeed came especially, to hear the ever evolving and exaggerated story of Terry Stubbles and the kidnapping, and Natalie delighted in telling it.

Come Halloween, it was actually Natalie's idea to invite Vince's nan to join them behind the bar to mix cocktails. The idea started from a plan to do a happy hour half-price Bloody Mary. However, having both tried to mix a Bloody Mary, and deciding that it tasted all wrong, Natalie leapt on the opportunity to recruit Vince's nan for the evening. Vince was not at all keen on the plan. Although he could accept that his nan had demonstrated certain talents in that arena, other necessary bar-keeping talents, including polite and local-customer-based politically-neutral banter, were also a requirement. This, he was aware, would be lacking. However, Vince decided to humour Natalie anyway.

Ever since the infamous Terry Stubbles incident, Natalie had seemed more emotionally vulnerable than usual, and had started regularly asking for 'group hugs', even though there were only two of them to comprise the group. Vince had been increasingly concerned by this instability and worried that she might return to her carpet-lady phase.

An element of the new, emotionally expressive Natalie, which was beginning to really get on Vince's nerves, was that she had also started saying 'awrr bless' a lot. This was largely used in a show of empathy at others' misfortune, but without any effort to then assist the afflicted. A child in the park appears to have lost its mother: "awrr bless." An old lady is too frail to get up from the bench quickly enough and subsequently misses her bus: "awrr bless her." 'Awrr bless' was very much a distant and observational statement and didn't result in any notable effort to aid the victim that inspired it. Vince, however, saw it as a cry from Natalie for some empathy for herself, so tried his best to humour her. Ever since Natalie had recalled that Vince's nan had helped out at the bar buy handing out free and random cocktails, his nan had been thoroughly 'Awrr blessed', and Natalie had seemed keen to adopt his nan ever since.

Vince's nan was delighted at being called back for an encore of her drink-dispensing band night. She had subsequently insisted that Bloody Mary happy hour be extended to a 'Halloween Fancy Dress Cocktail Night' – the details of which had then failed to become apparent, other than his nan making a special trip to the library to carry out some research. Vince, however, understood with a sense of increasing concern that 'Halloween Fancy Dress Cocktail Night' gave his nan free-rein to mix whatever random, but lethal, mix of alcohol she was inspired to concoct, with very little consideration of the effect it would have on the customers or the actual price of making it.

Halloween arrived, and word of mouth had meant that the bar was buzzing in anticipation. The promise of random killer-cocktails based on the foundation of Vince's nan's previous venture behind the bar created sufficient intrigue to entice the locals away from their warm televisions. Despite his apprehensions, the first hour or so had gone quite well. Overall there had been limited randomness from Vince's nan, and most customers had shown the sense to avoid the large bowl of 'Ghoul-Slime Punch' at the end of the bar.

Having left his nan at one end of the bar in charge of mixing the Bloody Marys, Vince was busy at the other end, deep in conversation with a group of bar-proppers about the lemon and lime scented shaving foam that he'd just started using. He'd bought it by accident in the chemists thinking he'd picked up the standard budget supermarket-own. However, its lemony pungency had given him the convincing illusion that he was actually shaving with a scoop off the top of a lemon meringue pie. He had been quite tempted thereafter to take a piece from the top of one of Natalie's lemon meringue pies from the kitchen's dessert menu, to compare and contrast the sensation. It had since crossed his mind to evaluate whether it was actually possible to shave with it. However, he had yet to develop sufficient courage to do this, knowing the reaction Natalie would have to her culinary creation being used for such an infantile experiment. Not surprisingly, this was one of the more interesting discussions that would grace The Carrot and Jam Kettle that evening, and so several marginally bored people at the bar were listening in. This included a man with a piece of black paper rolled into a cone with a star drawn on it, claiming to be a wizard, and another man dressed as a pirate, for which Vince was mentally unable to make the Halloween connection, but didn't want to ask for fear of offending him. His wife seemed to be dressed as Mr Miyagi from the *Karate Kid* – which Vince was also struggling with from a Halloween conceptual stand point.

As it was both cocktail night and 'spooky fancy dress night', Vince had gone for a traditional approach of cutting a hole in the middle of a black sheet for his head to go through, and then cutting out two smaller arm holes. He had then bought a plastic wizards hat from the market to round things off. However, he had since removed the pointy hat after the second glass breakage behind the bar. It was just the wrong size in terms of poking into the pint-glass store above the bar when he bent forward to clear empty glasses.

Natalie, meanwhile, had made the most of the dressing-up opportunity, and had come to the party as a very elaborate and flamboyant she-devil. This involved a figure-hugging blood-red cocktail dress, with tresselling flame-things hanging off the bottom that dragged on the floor behind her. The dress also had enormous red bat wings sleeves of a similar flaming tresselly nature. She also had a large wig of long black hair with two red devil horns poking out the top.

Vince could at least understand the Halloween connection based on the devil horns. However, he was less concerned about her artistic relevance and more that she was a walking disaster waiting to happen. The combination of the dress plus tottering around in red boots with 2-inch stilettoes with the tresseling things catching beneath them, meant it was a wonder she was still on her feet. The bat wing sleeves, meanwhile, had already resulted in him replacing a number of cocktails that her sleeves had got caught up in as she swept dramatically through the bar delivering Halloween-based meals. These included delicacies such as pumpkin soup, and pumpkin bake served with ghosts made from mounds of mash potatoes with sultanas for eyes. (Natalie was quite pleased with the latter as, with a short julienne of carrot for a nose, they would also double as snowmen during the Christmas period.) Other than catching on everything she walked past, it was a wonder Natalie's ridiculous sleeves hadn't been set on fire from the gas rings as she was preparing these treats.

Vince's nan, meanwhile, had gone for a far more practical approach, and had come as Wonder-Woman.

It was just as the woman dressed as Mr Miyagi joined the conversation by considering the practicalities of using lemon-meringue to shave her leg and armpit hair, that Jenny Davis made her dramatic entrance.

Jenny Davis

A few days previously, Jenny Davis had been in the bar at The Carrot and Jam Kettle with a couple of her friends. Vince had felt an anxious pang when he'd realised she was sitting with them at the corner table. His last encounter with her involved him being thrown out of her bed when she realised that he was no longer gainfully employed. It had not been the most amicable of partings. However, Vince's concerns were immediately dissipated when she came up and greeted him like an old friend.

"Hi Vince. How have you been? You seem to be doing all right for yourself. I heard that you now run this place."

The warmth in her voice and the flirtation in her eyes meant that Vince's memory of prior financial-based rejections immediately evaporated from his consciousness, as if it had never happened. When scientists eventually finish their examination of human DNA, they will no doubt identify the strand that is responsible for this phenomenon.

"Quite a stroke of luck, Jen. I helped out a rich American with some family problems, and so he bought 'The Carrot' and put me in charge like. What can I get you?"

Jenny Davis ordered drinks for her and her mates and chatted away whilst Vince poured them. Vince helped carry the drinks to her table and then watched from the bar as she sat and quietly returned to small talk with her group. She was clearly still interested in him. Vince considered this turn of events. Where did it leave the trade-up plan? Trading-up meant moving on, not going backwards. To reignite something with Jenny meant going backwards along the trading route. However, his romantic interlude with Jenny had only been for one night, and trades were supposed to work in three-month blocks, so had it really counted?

Natalie had been observing the course of events, and had looked on disapprovingly, in a scathing type of way. She and Vince had shared a lot over recent months. Vince could now claim a deeper understanding of Natalie's' feelings towards her former marriage than Dennis Sedgwick ever could. In return,

Natalie was now well versed in Vince's adventures over the past year and his aims to better himself. She was, therefore, familiar with the previous Jenny Davis incident, so it was easy for her to see what Jenny was up to. If she was honest with herself, Natalie had become very close with Vince. This emotion had multiplied considerably since Vince had heroically rescued her from the clutches of Terry Stubbles, shortly before he was knocked down by a trumpet. Vince was now a big part of Natalie's life, and no one else would be getting their hands on him, especially that dumb, gold-digging blonde that was flirting with him in the bar.

Jenny Davis had politely returned her empty glass to the bar, she had a final short chat with Vince, and explained how she would be coming on Saturday to the Halloween fancy dress. This was good for Vince; it gave him a couple of days to work out how Jenny might fit into the grand plan of trading-up, if at all.

***

When Jenny Davis entered the Halloween cocktail party and removed her coat, a number of beer-goggles turned. Jenny's 'slutty witch' costume involved a very tight, black, PVC cat suit, high healed boots and a velvet witch's hat. She slinked her way to the bar, metaphorically sweeping aside various dropped jaws from her path as she did so. As if bewitched, Vince's legs slinked over to the other end of the bar to serve her.

"What cocktail do you recommend then, Vince?"

Her warm voice was as velvety as her hat, and time stood still whilst Vince's brain tried to re-boot.

"Yaw could try one of me nan's 'Bloody-Hells'. It's like a Bloody Mary, but a bit more purple."

This drink was one of a variety of previously unknown drinking experiences that Vince's nan had devilishly concocted. Her idea with the 'Bloody Hell' was that if it was a drink no one had heard of, then no one could make out she'd mixed it incorrectly. Despite its secret recipe, there were distinct elements of Bailey's cream, and Ribena. Vince's nan had been going for a purple alternative to a Bloody Mary as she felt it was a bit more gothic and therefore increasingly vampire-ish.

As Vince passed the drink across the bar, Jenny took both the drink and Vince's hand.

"Do you think I look pretty as a witch? I do hope so."

Natalie was at the end of the bar, still in scathing mode. At this point, she lost control, and her inner she-devil kicked in.

Ghoul-Slime Punch

'Ghoul-Slime Punch' is a very difficult cocktail to make. Consequently, Vince's nan had been working on it all afternoon. Of course, a woman of Vince's nan's experience can put together the key ingredients of a bowl of punch in a flash, and a pungent brew of rums, bourbons and grenadine had quickly been assembled. However, for 'Ghoul-Slime Punch', consistency is everything. Slime is less of a drink and more the epitome of a bad cold. Getting the essence of this requirement into the form of an alcoholic beverage is one of the biggest challenges a bartender can face. A bottle of blackcurrent cordial was the first sticky goo to be added. However, the effects of this, in terms of slime, were disappointing. After several other experimental additions, a large can of treacle was then stirred in to the mix as well. At a later stage, a reasonable helping of corn flour was poured in for good measure. The final addition of Sour-apple Schnapps was an attempt to make the resulting concoction a greener slime. Unfortunately this only added to the brownness already within. It did, however, add an interesting layer to the flavour. The thick, pasty liquid passed both the alcohol requirement and the slime consistency, and so colour would have to go by the wayside.

Trevor was the first to try the punch. This was largely because he had fallen asleep in a corner of the bar at lunch time and no one had had time to wake him up and throw him out. Therefore, when Vince's nan triumphantly entered the bar late afternoon with her large bowl of brown slime, he was the perfect guinea pig.

Never one to refuse a free drink, Trevor had greedily accepted the challenge. Once his subsequent coughing fit had ended, his feedback was two-fold. Firstly, he found that he had needed to drink it all in one go. This, considering its alcohol content, was not easy, and was largely because it lacked the key liquid qualities normally associated with a drink. Once the gelatinous goo had started slipping down his throat there was no way to stop it. His second observation was that rather than a festive punch, what Vince's nan had really come up with was a heavily alcoholic glue.

The punch had since tempted limited takers, and had remained almost as a display piece on the bar until the time that

Jenny Davis made her entrance. It was this very same, largely untouched, heavily alcoholic glue that Natalie instinctively reached for as her weapon of choice in her showdown with the cat-suited temptress.

"You leave him alone, you gold-digging bitch!"

In synchrony with her outburst, Natalie grabbed the large bowl of punch and swung it forward to release the content. The punch slipped freely forward in one huge gelatinous paste and connected squarely with Jenny's face. Having wrapped around her head sufficiently to knit her hair together, the Ghoul-Slime Punch then oozed down the front of her costume. Vince's nan looked on with a strong sense of pride at the authenticity, ooze-wise, of the slime she had created.

After the initial shock and stress at being slimed with Ghoulish punch, Jenny Davis's response was to throw herself violently at Natalie. The two women crashed to the floor, gathering up various ash-trays, stools, empty glasses and bar snacks in Natalie's sleeves as they went.

Despite its early promise, it was one of the least dramatic bar fights witnessed in that part of the Midlands. Both contenders had started off in outfits that they were struggling to be mobile in, even whilst in a non-combat environment. In a conflict situation, their ability to move freely was even further inhibited. Add to this, the fact that they were now both glued together with the adhesive Ghoul-Slime Punch, and the freedom of movement needed to commit any kind of violence against each other was simply not available.

Vince looked on in horror as the two glued women struggled together on the floor, like twin butterflies trying to wriggle out of a cocoon. He had never been fought over before and was unsure of the protocol. Was he expected to intervene and stop the fight? Should he pick a side and shout encouragement to his favoured contestant? A final alternative was to wait for the outcome of the contest and then be claimed as a prize by the victor? The latter was obviously a choice more reserved for virginal medieval princesses waiting to be rescued and married off. However, these were enlightened post-feminist times and Vince decided not to be hasty and rule anything out.

Fortunately, whilst Vince was floundering with indecision, his nan had swooped decisively from behind the bar and was in the process of pulling a frantically arm-swinging Jenny Davis from off the top of Natalie. This was not an easy task, taking into consideration the lack of flexibility in the outfit and the amount of adhesive punch involved. Eventually, with some assistance from both Trevor and Vince finally deciding to join in and pulling back Natalie, the two were parted. This was accompanied by a large tearing sound as a she-devil bat-wing and a black curly wig became securely installed on the front of Jenny Davis.

"Yaw can get out of this pissin' pub right now! Coming in here, starting fights!"

The pub fell silent as Vince's nan motioned dramatically towards the door and a fuming Jenny Davis skulked out of the pub, looking and feeling considerably less glamorous than when she had entered. Whilst it might be assumed that Vince's nan dishing out orders would be undermined by the fact that she was in a slightly inappropriate Wonder-Woman costume for a person of her significant years, it actually seemed to help underpin her authority.

"Vince, you take Natalie upstairs and sort this out. I'll look after the bar whilst you're gone. Stu can come and help to clean this up."

Stu Nevis was the new kitchen hand. At the start of the management partnership, Vince and Natalie had agreed that they would manage the bar and kitchens on their own. The bar meals were mainly deep fried frozen food with a salad garnish, and they usually only did about twenty to thirty meals on a good night. So, stacking the washing-up machine hadn't been a taxing addition to the daily routine. However, in recent months, Natalie had been getting in to her home-made bar meals. These were created in the afternoon before the evening shift, and seemed to generate an inordinate amount of washing up. Also, since band night, Natalie had spent quite a bit more time in the bar talking to punters. These two factors combined to create a need for a washer-upper. Stu was the nephew of long-standing bar-propper, Trevor. He was a lad of sixteen who had recently left school with a small collection of low-grade GCSEs and no ambitions, drive, or career prospects.

Stu felt that the responsibility of his poor start to adult life should be shared equally by himself and his former school. He had undergone years of academic instruction for which he had little ability or interest. The school's aim was not to prepare him for his adult life, but to get their averages up on maths and sciences, so as to have a higher rating than the school in the next suburb along. Therefore, the only career-advice on offer to Stu was to continue into the sixth-form with more maths and sciences, and if that was not your thing you simply stepped out of the system with low grades and low prospects.

Of course, like all kids, Stu could have spent less time watching TV and getting his homework done. However, in his view, if you don't understand what's going on, doing homework badly to demonstrate this is the case isn't going to contribute much to getting a job you've not yet heard of, and wouldn't get anyway. Subsequently, news of a washing up job at The Carrot and Jam Kettle solved a number of immediate problems for Stu. It was at least a job, and prevented the need to apply for other jobs for which he was neither qualified, nor experienced, or even aware that they existed.

Stu had a very ordinary and quiet demeanour, which meant that he largely passed through life unnoticed. This was the case as he scrubbed brown slime from the bar-room floor, as punters enjoying the party flowed around him to socialize, noticing his red bucket of soapy water more than they noticed him.

Following the sage instructions from his aging, Superhero-nan, Vince had reluctantly done as he was told. If it was the choice between trying not to say the wrong thing to a distressed goop-covered she-devil, or making sure his nan didn't destroy his bar whilst left alone for ten minutes, the later was by far the preferable option. Despite this, he took the distressed woman to the flat above the bar and sat her next to him on the sofa. He put a tentative arm on her shoulder. Instinctively he knew she probably wanted a 'group hug', but the full extent to which she was now covered from head to toe in Ghoul-Slime Punch was surprising, considering how gloopy and un-flowing it had originally seemed. It was also a bit whiffy. There was no need for Vince be caked in it as well.

"I'm so sorry. I've really embarrassed us Vince, but I did that for you. Yaw must know that."

As she spoke, Natalie started sobbing and threw herself into a gluey embrace around Vince.

"I care about you too much to let that bloomin' gold-digger take advantage of you, Vince."

Vince took a moment to gather his thoughts.

"It's alright, Nat. When I started out with this 'trading-up' business, I was trying to make myself the sort of successful man that I thought the Jenny Davis types in this world would take seriously, and be attracted towards me. Now that I am becoming more successful I've realised that I daw want anything to do with that sort of person."

Natalie looked up and gave Vince a short but very sticky kiss. To Vince's surprise, he then kissed her back.

Chapter 7 – New Year's Eve

Broadening horizons

New Year's Eve had suddenly become stressful. It had promised to be a busy night as The Carrot and Jam Kettle was gaining popularity based on its new reputation for obscure-but-entertaining incidents of mild violence. However, two days before the arrival of the big night, Vince had received a call from Fairchild.

Vince's last interaction with the Fairchild clan was back in August, when Susan had sent him copies of the paperwork for the ownership and management of the pub. Since that time there had been no contact between them at all. This would normally seem a little strange for two parties who had just gone into business together. Vince was not surprised in the least, though.

Setting up Vince in the pub had been used by Susan as a way of impressing her new and very rich American. Fairchild believed that Vince had saved the day on a pony trek, and this had helped his new family to bond. However, by helping out Vince, Susan was really ingratiating herself to Fairchild. The second bird to be hit by this same convenient stone was that the business venture had put many miles between herself and her new family, and Vincent. Vince suspected that this might link back to the time when he worked for her at her hotel in Paddington and the kitchens were blown up, but he couldn't be sure.

A lot had happened in Vince's life since their last meeting. The band night; cocktail night; the ebb and flow of Natalie's emotional rollercoaster; Vince's nan joining in behind the bar. Fairchild, meanwhile, had not managed to go incident-free either.

Fairchild's daughter, Emily, had headed to Paris, and was soon sending back greetings from the capital of culture. She reported to be getting on well, and experiencing the broadening of the mind that travel can bring. She had made a new friend in the French capital and was happy there. Days were reportedly spent in and out of museums and art galleries, whilst evenings of drinking coffee in corner cafes debating philosophy and drinking in the beauty of Parisian life were the norm.

Fairchild was delighted, it was yet another success as a result of his 'Zapata Theory' (which dictates that a brief vacation involving a horse will solve all lingering family problems). Not only was he deeply gullible when it came to his daughter, he was also getting a little bored with suburban monotony himself. Vince, his former chauffeur, was off with the new challenge of running his traditional English pub, and Emily was off adventuring in uncharted corners of darkest Europe. Fairchild, meanwhile, was skulking in Richmond inactivity to avoid a number of London social circles who had yet to forget his misjudged enterprise involving the removal company he'd supplied the trucks for, and the subsequent highly publicised antiques heist.

Fairchild decided that it was time to get some distance from all of this tedium. The need for a new adventure had arrived, and he announced this to Susan one breakfast time. This was shortly after reading a second letter from Emily that explained how much she was loving France, and the sense of independence and maturity all this travelling was inducing in her. She gave her heart-felt thanks for him trusting her enough to embrace this rite of passage in her own independent way. Fairchild announced that it was time that he and Susan toured around Europe as well.

Susan was aghast at the suggestion that their lives lacked adventure. Their most recent adventure of a holiday to Wales was still haunting many of her waking moments. Despite this, she had finally netted her millionaire, and got him all to herself. The annoying spoiled daughter was now well out of the way, and that brummie-sounding little toad was now at arm's length as well. She was still concerned that in his ignorance, Vincent might inadvertently blurt out something about the illegal workforce that had almost been blown-up at the same time that he'd decided to ignite her hotel in Paddington. Fairchild was a very moral man, and that kind of information might be difficult for him to un-hear.

Susan also knew well enough that travelling around Europe in autumn and winter had the potential to be as cold and miserable as staying still in Europe, which included Richmond. Besides, there was every chance that Fairchild would want to visit Emily early on in the journey, and clearly neither of the women in his life wanted that. It was this in-depth analysis that prompted Susan to suggest an alternative: travelling around South East Asia.

Her arguments were threefold. Firstly, the two of them deserved a luxury holiday, but just the two of them, away from everything else. It has been a stressful time so early on in their relationship, what with the hotel fire, the antiques heist, and Emily, and pony-trekking. Now it was a time for just the two of them. Secondly, Susan pointed out that Fairchild was a man who loved his history. Asia was full of it: great walls, temples, monks, pottery statues, big golden Buddhas, more temples, more monks. Also, Asian history had the big advantage of it rarely being located in a thick shroud of dull and damp drizzle. Thirdly, Fairchild was a well-respected and successful businessman. These days in the global village, the place to do business was Asia.

Fairchild had been easily convinced. They had started their tour in Singapore. They then moved on to Bangkok. From there they became a little more adventurous and descended from the steps of smaller aeroplanes onto runways in the territories of Vietnam and Cambodia. After this, they reduced their adventurousness and hired a large yacht stocked with expensive wines and a full crew, and floated around the Gulf of Thailand for a month. Much as the latter gave Fairchild a chance to dive into crystal clear ocean waters, sunbathe on deserted beaches and spend 'quality-time' with Susan, there were a number of additional outcomes. With a drive and passion, equal only to his recent dabblings in the house-removal trade, Fairchild decided that he was going to start investing in businesses in Asia. Yachts, diving schools, guest-houses, monorails, deep-sea drilling, and that sort of thing.

A second outcome was that Fairchild got so drunk on the yacht with expensive wines one night that he accidentally proposed to Susan. Susan had also been particularly amorous in the preceding days, which could largely be put down to her being the only woman on a boat filled with men in sailor uniforms. Despite the distractions, she was not one to miss an opportunity when it arose. Within four days she had managed to organise a legally binding shot-gun style wedding on a beach in Thailand. This was achieved with support from an orange-robed monk that acted as both the priest and Fairchild's best man, and a number of lady-boys who enthusiastically played the role of bridesmaids on condition they got to keep the outfits afterwards. They were clearly those amongst the available population who were prepared to put some passion and effort into the event, so added greatly to proceedings. Fairchild had been dressed up to look like a dignitary from an eighteenth century French infantry regiment, where the Parisian uniform designer had been given far too much artistic freedom and had then blown the entire budget on the first outfit. Susan had looked glamorous in various kitch and floaty numbers, with theatrical make-up applied so thickly that Fairchild found it difficult to tell who she was. It was of no consequence to Susan. She was now Mrs Jonathan Fairchild, and the British High Commission had documents in duplicate to prove it. Not only had the metaphoric fly been stuck to the web, but he was now at the stage of becoming liquefied tissue for easy digestion.

Fairchild's final additional outcome of the great South East Asian tour was his post-marriage decision to be photographed with a genuine Indochinese tiger. He had seen a programme about wildlife sanctuaries on cable TV when staying in a hotel room in Bangkok. The lucky visitors with the right credit cards got to meet a tame tiger face to face, helped to take it on a bit of a walk and then be photographed together. It solved the question of what to put on the first personalised Christmas cards that they would send out from the new Mr. and Mrs. Fairchild.

Fairchild had over-looked that the specialist animal sanctuaries featured on the TV would have highly skilled handlers, and tigers that are sensitised to interact with people from when they are young cubs. The slightly run down Cambodian animal sanctuary where Fairchild chose to achieve his new whim did not really fall into that category. It was one containing a couple of previously ensnared and rather fed-up wild tigers in a cage. Had Fairchild investigated further, he would have found that the attempts from the tigers' keepers to instil basic social skills in their current charges could, at best, be considered minimal. The staff member, who was responsible for lobbing meat over the top of the netting once a day to nourish the depressed animals, couldn't believe his luck. A crazy, ankle-sock clad American had turned up declaring he would pay good money to actually go inside the tiger enclosure for a photo with them. It was money for nothing.

It was, therefore, not so much a decision to return to London as it was his urgent need to be medivaced that determined the resumption of life in Fairchild's Richmond home. Having rested and healed up, his thoughts turned to his affairs in England, and more importantly the desire for a pint of ale in a traditional English pub. Of course, he might as well have the fun of doing this in the pub that he already owned. The photo that resulted might also make a more appropriate Christmas card for the following year. He'd been forced to send conventional cards this year, as the blurry images of orange stripes, claws, teeth, blood and ankle socks, that Susan had taken were not really what he had been going for. Therefore, he phoned up Vince and told him to expect his employer to visit The Carrot and Jam Kettle on New Year's Eve.

New Year's Eve... again

Stu Nevis was in the kitchen, re-loading the dishwasher. Lukewarm water poured from the tap into the large industrial sink in preparation for the next round of endless saucepan scrubbing. The emersion-heater in the flat above had not kept pace with the washing-up needs on this busy night. On a couple of occasions, Stu had boiled extra water using one of the gas stoves, but had since become resigned to the fact that plunging his hands yet again into cold water on this wintery night and scrubbing a bit harder would probably improve his chances of getting out of the kitchen before midnight.

His boss's partner, Natalie, seemed to be obsessed about the cleanliness of kitchen sinks, and so he'd needed to scrub them harder than the saucepans if he was to be given permission to finish up for the night. If he did a good job, he might even go into the bar and try to get a free drink out of the boss, Mr Crow.

The boss-man seemed a bit stingy to Stu, always checking up on things and trying not to spend any money on the place. However, it was New Year's Eve so there was a small chance that a more generous side of the man would shine through. Stu may well have been young, but he was not so wet behind the ears to realise that Uncle Trevor was unlikely to get a round in, despite the New Year spirit of good will.

The washing machine clunked back into action. Stu pushed a large tray welded with the crusted black remnants of a steak and ale pie into the soapy depths of cold water and shivered as his hand followed in afterwards. There had to be more to life than washing up. Even if his school had failed to inform him about possible careers that might have suited him, they could at least have warned him to avoid ones like this. The cold of the greasy water seemed to heighten Stu's senses. It was time for him to make his New Year's resolution. He had to make a change. He would resolve to do all he could to find a job that didn't require him to scrape congealed, sooted gunk from the back of the oven once a week, or empty the u-bend beneath the sinks where the rotting vegetable chunks and abandoned bits of un-chewable fat from the edges of cheap steaks accumulated.

As Stu Nevis silently swore an oath to his new resolution, party poppers and whoops of delight could be heard from the bar, as the clock struck midnight and a new year began. A chorus of 'Auld Lang Syne' pre-empted the playing of the conga. If you hadn't already had the opportunity to grab someone and snog them as midnight was proclaimed, then a second chance to grab someone presented itself as you watched their rear end wiggle out of time to the music of Black Lace. Participants drunkenly snaked their way with others in a similar state to previously unexplored corners of the bar-room in the hope that further snogging opportunities remained before the night disintegrated into a drunken and regrettable haze.

In the bar, it had been Natalie that Vince had snogged on the stroke of midnight. It was also Natalie whose waist Vince had grasped as they did the conga through the lounge room; such was the depth of his commitment to the woman.

Since Halloween in fact, Vince and Natalie had expressed their feelings for each other and had gone a bit over the top. Vince was determined to be a better man than Dennis Sedgwick, and had set about proving this by regularly buying small but tacky gifts for Natalie. Natalie was concerned that she had to ensure Vince wouldn't stray off. She was well aware of how the three-month trade-up scheme worked and was determined that she would not be dumped after that time when Vince decided that it was time to move on again. She, too, had therefore invested in a number of tacky gifts for Vince. Consequently the front room of the flat was starting to look like the plastic tat shelf in a pound shop.

Stu scrubbed half-heartedly at the final pan and then emptied the sink. He used the handle of a dessert spoon to get the majority of damp leftovers out of the plug hole and then squeezed a good helping of washing-up liquid around the sink before returning to his scrubbing. This would definitely be the last New Year's Eve that he would ever be doing this, he decided. From tomorrow he was going to start looking for a better job. This time next year he would be having fun as part of the conga, not the one in the back trying to sand-down the sinks with a worn out Brillo Pad.

Arrival

Fairchild had arrived at The Carrot and Jam Kettle at around half past eight. After a warm greeting and a warm pint, Natalie had shown him to the spare room that she'd made up for him above the pub. Mrs Fairchild had chosen to remain in Richmond, giving the excuse that she needed to help the gardener plan where the tulip bulbs needed to be planted so that they would be ready for the coming summer. Fairchild was delighted that she was so keen to help feather their family home, and conceded that it was probably more important that she should stay in London.

Having settled in, Fairchild made his way downstairs to the bar. His aim of course was to recreate the success of his night in the Welsh tavern and entertain the clientele of The Carrot and Jam Kettle with tales of his recent adventures. He looked around for the gathering of locals that were desperate for a well-travelled and entertaining man like himself to brighten their day. Unfortunately, this 'traditional English pub' experience did not meet with his romantic expectations: the roaring fire in the hearth; locals in grubby work clothes spilling beer amongst the sawdust; landed gentry in their tweeds comparing pheasant shooting stories. All of these staple requirements of an authentic English ale-house were missing. The reality was a room heaving with tarted-up women yelling drunkenly at loud-shirt clad drunken men over the booming dance music. On the periphery were a few older men who had braved the event in the hope of a snog beneath the mistletoe once the level of drunkenness amongst the tarted-up women reached a suitable peak. In the meantime they were yelling at each other about the third round of the FA cup. Who amongst these outcasts would be drawn in to hear a tale of a man who had recently and heroically survived a vicious tiger mauling? As things stood, Fairchild was completely unable to spot his captive audience.

Fairchild was so disheartened that he had considered going back up to his room, even before seeing in the New Year. As this thought entered his mind, he was approached by Vince's nan and Trevor.

"Yaw-right there Mr Fairchild? Vince said you would be coming up. London can be too crowded at this time of year. I went down on the train to do Christmas shopping once. Pissin' with rain it was. And the prices! A box of chocolates from Oxford Street was more pissin' expensive than all the Christmas shopping I'd normally do in a year. You're better off getting the cut-price chocolate eggs after Easter and saving them up. Last Easter Mrs Barry next door came out in a nut allergy and they had to getting the pissin' ambulance men round. They couldn't get her out of the door on the pissin' stretcher cos she'd just had the builders in. All the dust sheets and off-cuts were piled up in the hallway from the week before when they'd been re-doing the architraving. Pissin' cowboys!"

"And I'm Trevor."

Having added in this much-needed annex to the formalities, Trevor then realised that no introductions had been decanted in the first place, and so hastily added the missing introductions as well.

"This is Vince's nan by the way, Mr Fairchild. Perhaps you'd like to join us for a chat and we can tell you all about the area and the history of the place. Mine'll be a pint of bitter."

Fairchild obligingly ordered a round of drinks and they found a quieter corner at the back of lounge area from which to share their fascinating stories. As the conversation followed, Fairchild became acutely aware that the area and local history held very little interest for him. It was true that he enjoyed history, and was passionate for the history of revolutionaries and horses, like Zapata and his flamboyant moustache, up-holding his morals with the haciendas.

In contrast to this colourful legend, Trevor's local historic account was one of drudgery. It started with the pre-war drudgery of his grandfather in the grimy factory at the end of the grimy street. Next was the war-time drudgery of his father at war whilst his mum worked in the grimy factory. This was followed up with Trevor's factory-based post war drudgery, and then his nephew, Stu's, contemporary drudgery. The drudgery timeline was generously punctuated by Vince's nan, with anecdotal accounts of the various illnesses and diseases of relatives and neighbours. The combination of her limited medical understanding and sketchy memory did nothing to lighten the overall tale. Fairchild gradually reached the conclusion that people in this part of the world actually enjoyed their drudgery. It was New Year's Eve and they were down the pub at a party. The conversation he was stuck in was more appropriate for a counselling session for the terminally depressed than for an end of year celebration.

By two o'clock, Fairchild's mind was long since made up. He no longer wanted to be the owner of a suburban Midlands pub. It was nothing at all like it was supposed to be. He wanted to be greeted by all as an old friend as he entered the bar. His anecdotes needed to be heard enthusiastically by bearded farmhands, chewing thoughtfully on a piece of straw as they listen to Fairchild and waited for their ploughman's lunch to be served. The friendly locals would then amuse him with the comic tales of events about working class mishaps. All of this, The Carrot and Jam Kettle, was not.

Fairchild's plan

Fairchild watched as Vince assisted the final drunken reveller out of the pub and slid the bolts at the top of the double doors into place. Natalie had already gone to bed. The deal was that Vince would lock up, but she would try to rise a bit early and start on the hoovering and mopping so they could open for lunch time.

"Not a bad night, Mr Fairchild. We should have made quite a bit of money there. People seemed to enjoy themselves which will go towards making the pub more popular as time goes on."

From his bar-stool, Fairchild beckoned Vince to come and join him. Vince walked behind the bar, and reached for a twelve year old malt and two glasses. He placed them in front of Fairchild and then pulled up a bar-stool that he kept at the back of the bar. He knew that Fairchild enjoyed a scotch. He also knew that he needed to manage Fairchild throughout the visit. Susan may not appreciate Vince. However, so long as Fairchild still considered him the hero of the Welsh pony-trekking adventure and the man who was making him money at The Carrot and Jam Kettle, then Vince would be fine.

"You know Vince, this is not what I imagined an English pub would be like."

Vince poured them a double scotch each before replying.

"There are lots of pubs in England that look different from the outside. People had fun tonight that's the main thing. They spent their money, had a drink, and forgot for a few hours about the boring work that they do, and how things could have worked out better. It's not that different really. It's the people inside that make the pub, and most people are there to escape other things. Anyway, it's not always loud like it was tonight. New Year's is a bit special. In the week it's usually just a bunch of men like Trevor, talking about football or the good old days."

Fairchild sipped at his scotch whilst his mind recalled the recent explanation of the good old days from Trevor. It did not inspire a sudden change of heart for The Carrot and Jam Kettle.

"Well Vince, I've just come back from Asia. I have decided to invest over there. The opportunities are huge. They want our business you see. It only takes a few days to set up a business once you pay the right people. In the West it can take months to get permits, planning permission, and set up HR and finance systems to meet all the regulations. After that, half of what you profit is tax anyway. Over there it's easy. If you've got the capital to invest you can't go wrong."

Vince looked back at Fairchild, listening intently. He wasn't sure where this was going, but it didn't sound good.

"I'm going to sell up The Carrot and Jam Kettle, Vince. It's time to look at bigger and better things. Something that can grow; has room for expansion."

Vince downed the remainder of his scotch. His previous changes under the trade-up scheme had been either his own decision, or the result of some disaster outside of his control. The selling of The Carrot and Jam Kettle was neither. He had expected some kind of congratulations or a bonus for making such a good job of it. But not this.

"When do you think you'll sell up, Mr Fairchild? Perhaps you can give me a bit of time to find something else first?"

Fairchild smiled at Vince with a fatherly grin.

"It seems you've missed the point, Vince. I want you to manage a guesthouse for me out there. In Asia. It'll be a good quality place, but made to look like a traditional English guesthouse. The bar will be all wooden panelling, decked in shire-horse equipment and paintings of fox-hunting. We'll import a few English bitters and stouts, as well as more drinkable European beers. You'll run the show Vince, and if we set it up well, we'll find a new manager to keep it going. Then you'll start another one until we have a chain of them."

Vince had never been to Asia. When he was a kid, his nan had used to keep a small snow globe on her dresser that doubled as a globe of the world, with the snowy liquid behind the continents being the oceans that became a bit rough, indeed snowy, as it was shaken. As a concept it was marginally flawed, however it did mean that Vince could appreciate that Asia was quite a big place in comparison to England. He regretted that Fairchild wasn't being a bit more specific. A beach hut in Bali and a posting in Vladivostok could both fall within the same broad 'Asia' category. Vince slowly took on board the scant information that he had, and considered it in terms of trade-ups.

He had set himself the task of a trade-up every three months. This was to trade his life forward to bigger and better things: the job, the girl, the wheels, the pad, and the threads. He poured himself a second drink. Staring hard into the depth of his twelve year old malt he briefly thought about what he had achieved:

Trade one had been the barman job at The Carrot and Jam Kettle. This initial but brief move had included a one night stand with Jenny Davis, and possibly something magical with Natalie Sedgwick, should either of them ever manage to recall what on earth happened.

Trade two had been at the factory. It wasn't much of a step up, and he'd blown it anyway when he'd tried to move beyond the mindless elements of his task and introduce his out-sourcing idea. However, it had been where he had met Kaleena, and that had led to trade-up number three.

Trade three had seen him working as receptionist in a London hotel, still with Kaleena. Again there had been positive and negative elements to this experience, but his eventual departure had been under something of a cloud.

Trade four he was a driver, eventually for Fairchild, and had spent many an evening in the company of Emily buzzing around in a newly bought Porsche.

Trade five brought him back to The Carrot and Jam Kettle, this time as its manager, and he and Natalie had eventually got together.

So, timing aside, he had pretty much achieved more than he had set out to in terms of the job, the girl, the wheels, the pad and the threads. Four complete trade-ups had been the aim for year one. In fact he had achieved five different types of employment, four romantic encounters; two cars (if you counted the Polonez), five different living quarters including his nans, and a range of acceptable threads, – chauffeur uniform aside. Even now he was sitting having a drink with Fairchild, being offered yet another chance of what could be a bigger and better trade-up.

Following his mental review of year one, Vince asked himself the question: *Was it still necessary to keep trading his life every three months?* 'Trading Vincent Crow' had got him this far, but was it time to step back from that and make the most of what it had brought him? He and Natalie had made a good go of the pub.

Maybe they could take out a mortgage and buy the property from Fairchild. Vince had made it far further up the ladder in one year than he'd ever dreamed was possible. Perhaps on that basis there was some room for a few rule changes to the trading system.

"Yaw know what, Mr Fairchild. It sounds like a very interesting idea, going to Asia and then starting up a guesthouse."

Vince paused while he double checked in his mind that he was doing the right thing. It would mean the end of the trade-up plan.

"It'll have to be arranged so that Natalie comes along as well. Oh, and thinking about it, can me nan come too?"